VANISHED

A LUCA MYSTERY CRIME THRILLER

A LUCA MYSTERY
BOOK 2

DAN PETROSINI

Print ISBN: 978-1-960286-04-8

Naples, FL

Library of Congress Control Number: 2023901504

OTHER BOOKS BY DAN

Complicit Witness

Push Back

Ambition Cliff

ACKNOWLEDGMENTS

Special thanks to Julie, Stephanie and Jennifer for their love and support, and thanks to Squad Sergeant Craig Perrilli for his counsel on the real world of law enforcement. He helps me keep it real.

1

STEWART

"No amount of travel on the wrong road will bring you to the right destination." - Ben Gaye, III

MAY 3RD

I shifted in my chair as Kevin Greely made his case to our largest client. They had a huge contract for a desalination plant we wanted, no, we needed, but I couldn't help thinking my boss's groveling was sickening. My phone vibrated again, the third time in five minutes. I glanced around the table. All eyes were fixed on the PowerPoint presentation, so I dipped into my jacket for a peek. Frozen, I stared at the number as it buzzed.

It was her.

I pushed back from the conference table, drawing the attention I dreaded.

"Uh, sorry. I gotta get this. Family emergency. I'll be right back."

Greely's eyes bore into me as he said, "Hustle up, Dom, we're moving to your wheelhouse next."

"This should only take a minute." Slinking out of the

room, I knew I'd have to concoct something believable to keep Greely off my back. Boy, did I hate kissing ass. This job was nothing special, just a placeholder, and the money sucked to boot. I had to move on, and fast.

Hitting callback, I hunched near a column with my eyes on the conference room door.

"Dom?"

A shiver, part exhilaration, part queasiness, ran from my gut to my nose. I felt like a fifth grader calling my crush from the bathroom. The quote, "Good things come to those who wait," rushed into my head.

"Hey, Robin, sorry, I was in a—"

"Phil's still not back. Do you know where he is?"

"You sure?"

"He didn't come home again last night and didn't show up at work today. Where is he?"

She needed reassuring, and I was gonna provide it.

"I'm sure he'll be back—"

"Cut the bullshit, Dom, you said that yesterday. Where the hell is he?" She sounded frantic.

"I don't know, Robin."

"Oh, come on, he tells you everything."

Spot-on. "Look, I'm sure he's okay, but did you check around, like the hospitals?"

"Of course. I checked NCH Downtown and North, Lee Memorial, Health Park, even Physicians Regional, though he'd never go there. Something's wrong, I can feel it."

I had to agree with her. "I'm sure there's an explanation. You've got to remain calm. Let's not jump to any conclusions here. Okay, Robin?"

"I know, but look, you can tell me. I just wanna know." She raised her voice. "Is Phil screwing around again? Has he taken off with another one of his bimbos?"

I didn't need to be reminded that Phil collected women like coins. The crazy thing was, it was nuts to do so, given he had Robin.

Robin and Phil had been married for ten years, some good, some bad. I remember the day they got hitched. Robin was a catch: good-looking and making serious money at only twenty-five. That wedding day was bittersweet for me because Phil, was a life-long friend, the brother I never had. The two of them made such a striking couple it was depressing.

My buddy, Phil Gabelli, was no slouch either, and I hated competing with him for girls as we grew up. The fact is, I never stopped competing with him. Even married to Robin he was still dipping his beak in where I fished. He had Robin, I mean, what the hell else could you want?

The conference door groaned open and a stern-faced Greely said,

"You're up Stewart!"

I held up a finger. Greely shook his head, hiked his thumb, and disappeared. Man, I can't wait to tell these guys to go fuck off.

"Look, Robin, I know you're upset, but I'm sure he'll turn up. He always does."

"I don't know what to do, Dom. This time is different, I can feel it."

I could hear her cell phone ringing in the background.

"Don't worry—"

"Hold on a sec. Oh, I gotta go. It's the detective handling the case."

Detective? Case? Do detectives get involved in a missing persons report? I reached for my inhaler. It was probably normal. Robin was a type A. It was one of things I loved about her, though Phil didn't feel the same way. She'd push

9

with a laser-like focus, bullying you or turning on the charm, either way, whatever worked, to get what she wanted. Phil would complain to me about it, but I knew it was the reason she was so successful. He didn't know how to handle her, but I found her easy to deal with. Like I told Phil, putting up with her foibles was a small price to pay for all the dough she brought in.

2

STEWART

"If you can find a path with no obstacles, it probably doesn't lead anywhere." - Frank A. Clark

LOOKING IN THE MIRROR, MY FIVE-O'CLOCK SHADOW bothered me. I shaved and put on a nice pair of jeans and a new shirt I'd gotten at a Waterside boutique. I wanted to look upscale casual, whatever that meant, because a detective by the name of Frank Luca was coming by.

Luca was about six feet tall and good-looking, like Phil. I immediately wondered what Robin thought of him.

I went to shake his hand, but he waved his ID and stepped in.

"This shouldn't take long, just trying to get some background on Mr. Gabelli."

"No problem, Officer, or is it Detective? How should you be addressed?"

"Well, if my old man was here he'd say call me anything, but make the check out to cash." Luca smiled. "Detective, Officer, Frank, makes no difference."

"Sure. Is your pop still around?"

Luca shook his head. "Nah, been about five years now. Still tough to believe."

"Yeah, I know what you mean. I lost my mom two years ago and it still hurts. I like what Queen Elizabeth said, 'Grief is the price we pay for love.' Pretty good, isn't it?"

Luca nodded and pulled a notebook out of his jacket.

"Shall we get started?"

I pulled out a couple of bottles of water and we sat around the kitchen table.

"Crazy that Phil took off, ain't it?"

"You say took off, did he have any particular reason to run?"

"Well, you know, Phil was, I don't know, restless. He couldn't sit still for a minute, unless it was on a barstool chatting up a lady." I smiled.

"Phil liked to drink, womanize?"

"Well, he didn't drink that much. Look, me and Phil go way back. I mean, we're tight as can be. He's pulled me out of so many jams I lost count. I just don't want to bad-mouth him or nothing."

"I get it. I'm just trying to get some information to go on. Anything you tell me stays with me. I need to understand if he took off or if something happened to him."

I leaned forward. "What do you mean? Like he's hurt or—"

Luca threw up a palm. "Let's not get carried away. My job is to investigate his whereabouts and follow the leads, bad or good, wherever they point. Now, you were saying your buddy liked to play the field."

I smiled. "Fair enough, though not fair to Robin. She's something, ain't she?" I wanted Luca to react, but he didn't give me any clue to what he thought of her.

"Well, Phil's one of a kind. Let's say he's never had a

problem with the ladies. I'm sure you know what that's like, right Detective? I mean, with your looks. Hey, you know what?" I snapped my fingers. "You look like George Clooney. Yeah, that's it. Wow, a spitting image. You must get that a lot."

Luca smiled thinly and shook his head. What a stiff.

He said, "Go on."

"Let's just say Phil took full advantage of his situation. That's all."

"His situation?"

"You know, his looks, his way with women. You could call it style. He basically was irresistible."

"And did his wife know about his," Luca made quotation marks in the air, "activities?"

I frowned. "Yeah, she knew. Robin would get pissed and threaten to throw him out, but Phil'd weasel his way back in, making the same old promises. Robin would fall for it over and over."

"You think maybe she finally got tired of being made a fool?"

"What? You don't think? Nah, can't be, there's no way she'd do anything bad to anyone, not to Phil, no one."

"Got to ask."

"Yeah, I know most times it's the spouse, but hey, he's probably just," I lowered my voice a notch, "holed up with some kitten."

"Robin said you and Phil were tight as can be and if anyone knew where he was it would be you."

Robin? He's on a first-name basis with her already?

"Yeah, me and Philly go all the way back to grammar school. We played Little League, went to high school together and all. Robin probably told you I was his best man at their wedding."

Luca nodded silently.

"But really, I don't know where he went. I wish I did."

"Do you know if they had any financial issues?"

I shook my head. "No way. Robin brings home the bacon, and a lot of it at that."

Luca asked, "Perhaps he had money problems of his own."

"Nah, she makes more than enough, and they share it."

"You know they pool their money?"

"Like I said, Phil tells me everything."

The detective nodded. "Do you know anything or any reason at all for him to disappear?"

"Not really. He's had a couple of flings that lasted a while, but I don't know, I guess he could've taken off with one of his babes. You know it wasn't the best of marriages, and he'd say he wanted to take off sometimes."

"Did you take him seriously, or was it something a lot of people fantasize about when they hit a rough patch?"

I shrugged. "I guess no more than the next guy."

Luca asked me to name any of Phil's current and former girlfriends I could remember. After scribbling in his note-book, Luca stood, signaling the chat was over. As I walked him to the door, he asked, "Is there anyone you know he had a beef with? Anyone that might have a reason to cause him harm?"

Finally, a good question. "Well, to be honest, Phil could be kind of a wise guy at times. He loved to bust balls. You know what I mean? Nothing really mean-spirited, but some-times people could take him the wrong way. You know?"

"Anyone you think might have took him the wrong way?"

I gave him a couple of names and he left.

3

LUCA

MISSING PERSON CASES AREN'T MY BAG, BUT SINCE THERE'S few homicides along Florida's Gold Coast, it was a break from running down burglaries. Most of these types of cases break down to either someone flying the coop or murder, which, like I say, is rare, especially in Naples. Chances were this guy would turn out to be a runner.

While I interviewed the wife, I couldn't imagine this guy Phil Gabelli taking off on her. The wife's name was Robin, and boy was she a beauty. The woman began to hypnotize me as we talked, until I realized she screamed type A, which shook off my hormonal instincts. You see, type A's think they're smarter than everyone else. They're also known to be fanatical planners. It makes them successful, but many times they're also the ones who think their meticulous planning will allow them to get away with a crime.

I reassessed things. She was pretty torn up, but something wasn't quite right. The wife was holding back, but was it just the normal personal stuff nobody gives us the first time or two, or something more sinister? She was hard to read. I'd need more face time, but it was early, and who knows, her hubby might show up any minute.

The wife was insistent that I go see her husband's lifelong buddy, a guy named Dom Stewart. Was this a classic diversion, or was this her really trying to get to the bottom of her husband's disappearance?

I looked at the pictures Gabelli's wife gave me. I don't swing from the other side of the plate, but there was no doubt this dude was pretty. Come on, buddy, talk to me. Where the hell are you? Why don't you give your wife a call?

Putting the photos aside, I finished filling out a missing persons report. Then I ran the friend, Dom Stewart, through the system. Nothing came up, not even a speeding ticket. A real altar boy.

The sun was shining onto my desk, so I adjusted the blinds. I'd only been in paradise for two years, and I needed every day of them to get over the loss of my partner and best friend, J. J. Cremora. These Southerners are a lot sharper than the rest of the country thinks, well, here at the sheriff's office anyway. After I'd gotten down here, they cycled me through a bunch of temporary partners, knowing I'd need time. Finally, they permanently paired me with Mary Ann Vargas, who, I had to admit, was a good cop. She happened to be on vacation at the moment, not that I needed my partner to chase this case down.

Picking at leftovers from last night's Cinco De Mayo meal, I updated the case file with the report and interview and uploaded a picture of the missing guy. Nothing else was pressing, so I called this Stewart guy and headed back into the sunshine.

STEWART LIVED IN NORTH NAPLES, in one of the hundreds of gated communities that I thought gave people a false sense of security. I couldn't imagine having kids and dealing with the K-Mart cops at the gates to drop and pick them up. On the plus side, Pelican Perch was another example of a beautifully manicured community that was bright and cheery.

Dom Stewart lived in a medium-sized, second-floor coach home. Everywhere else they're called townhouses. I figured this place went for about three hundred and fifty thousand. That's another thing, down here, everyone is real estate centric. I can't recall the last conversation where the price of a house didn't sneak into the chat. Me? Guilty as charged. I enjoyed talking about it as well.

Anyway, Stewart cranked the door of his coral pink home open a millisecond after I rang the bell. I never liked that when it happened; it made me suspicious. Stewart was about five feet ten, one sixty, with brown hair. He looked like a guy who'd be anal about his garage. You know them, they have the floor painted in a high gloss and everything's hung up, nothing on the floor.

Stewart was wearing a light blue button-down shirt and a pair of three-hundred-dollar jeans. Was he trying to make an impression for our chat, or was he just one of those neat freaks? I showed him my badge and we made our way to the kitchen. Boy, the place was clean but sparsely furnished and needed updating. I lowered my estimate to three twenty-five max.

Inspirational-type prints hung everywhere. "May you live all the days of your life." I had to read that one twice before I got it. *"Life isn't about finding yourself. Life is about creating yourself."* "Fortune favors the brave."

A magnet proclaiming *"Carpe Diem"* was on the refrigerator. Stewart opened it, revealing a shelf of water bottles lined up like soldiers, and grabbed two before sitting.

He didn't seem nervous, but he either loved to talk or was trying hard to make a connection with me. I'd have to keep this guy on track or I'd be here all day. I made a few notes along the way, but it was looking like good old Phil had taken off with another gal. A chick magnet it seemed.

It was interesting but not surprising to learn that Phil was a bit of a wiseass. When things come a little too easily, a lot of guys get overconfident and it rubs some of us the wrong way. Maybe he really ticked someone off. It wouldn't be the first time some Romeo got whacked for playing with some other guy's Juliet.

I replayed what Stewart had said about guys who didn't care for Phil's arrogance. He gave three names but was there was something in his body language when he mentioned this guy Turnberry?

4

STEWART

"Doing what you want to do is easy. Doing what you have to do is hard." – Larry Elder

ROBIN TEXTED ME RIGHT AFTER SEEING LUCA TO TELL ME she'd put together a search team. Can't say I was surprised; she wasn't one to sit on her hands. I was glad she texted me but miffed she didn't tell me in advance she was thinking of one. Either way, I was on my way, but there was no question, a search team felt strange, and I didn't want to participate.

Robin lived in a nice section of Pine Ridge Estates, where the lots were large and the houses ranged from a million and a half up to three and more. I liked it. It had a good location that had its own feel and the name had a nice, highbrow ring to it. Her house was worth over two million, I discovered when I looked it up.

When I pulled up to the house, the gray paver driveway was already filled with cars. A small crowd had gathered on the covered entryway of the house. I surveyed the house as I got out of the car. It was always perfectly manicured, and today was no different.

Robin, clipboard in hand, was standing in the doorway. I quickened my pace, toning down my smile as I nodded hellos and sidled up to her for a quick embrace. Her cell phone buzzed. Man, she smelled good.

Robin finished the call from a volunteer.

"What's the plan?" I asked.

"I can't wait for the police. They said they'd find him, but the thought of him lying somewhere hurt—I, I just couldn't bear it."

She teared up. I reached for her hand and gave it a squeeze.

I said, "So let's get looking then. Where to?"

"I don't know where to look first. It's overwhelming."

"I know, but one step at a time. How about we divide up and start with the parks and wooded areas."

She nodded. "Yeah, I told Marty and Joe to take a few of us and head to Wiggins Pass, Veterans, and Gordon. We've got to check around his job."

"Good places to look."

She said, "There's also a lot of undeveloped land by the Tech Park on Old Forty-one."

Her cell phone buzzed and she told the caller to get a few others together and to search for Phil and his car at Big Cypress Park in the Everglades. The park was a vast swamp with boardwalk access. They'd need a hundred people to check it all out. Man, this was going to be a long night.

I had zero interest in walking through any wooded areas and even less in trudging through some skanky swampland. Staying with Robin was my plan. As teams began to form, I told Robin, "Detective Luca came by to see me."

"Really? I'm surprised. He didn't seem too interested. What did he have to say?"

Not interested? He had to be interested at least in her.

"Not much, just asked a bunch of questions. I gave him as much information as I could."

"Like what?"

"You know."

"If I knew I wouldn't ask. Now come on, Dom."

"I mean, we both know Phil liked to, you know," I fingered quotation marks, "roam around. I just told him what I knew. That's all."

A volunteer came up and spoke with Robin.

"Okay, let's get going," Robin said.

"What do you mean?"

"Searching."

"You're not going, are you?"

"Of course. I can't just sit here."

"But you gotta stay here. You know, this is the, the command center."

"You think so?"

Bingo, she was listening to me already. "Of course. You're the perfect person to be running things from here."

She briefly smiled. "If you think so."

"Absolutely. We should both be here."

"No, no. You can't stay here, Dom. Nobody knows Phil like you do. You'd know where to look. Peg will stay with me."

Damn. Much as I wanted, I couldn't push back against the reasoning.

Off I went with ten other do-gooders who started calling Phil's name out before they got off Robin's driveway.

IT WAS muggy as all hell, and my shoes were caked with dirt. We must've walked ten frigging miles through the farmland south of Immokalee Road and Everglades Boulevard. Why anyone thought Phil would be out here was a mystery to me. I played my part, calling his name out every couple of minutes, but I knew it was futile. It was a drag and I had to keep reminding myself of the quote by Kaplan: "*If I am right about the big picture, I will be rewarded for my patience.*"

I was starting to get hungry. I called Robin three times as we trudged along, ostensibly to see if anyone had any news. Though she was definitely stressed, she still sounded like a glass of sugar water. I couldn't wait until all this was over.

The sun was sinking, and I suggested we circle to the right and head back. I was never so happy to see the daylight dissipate into a dishwater gray as we got back in our cars. Starving, I headed back to Robin's.

All the search teams had come back hours ago, but there were still a dozen people at Robin's house. Go home folks. Can't you see she needs time to unwind? Unfortunately, her sister, Peggy, who'd driven down from Savannah, was now staying with Robin.

They were twins, mentally speaking, but Peg was nothing to look at, though she did have some money. I figured she'd be around for four, five days max, as she had a big job running a chain of hospitals. Robin said the two of them were no longer close, but blood is thick, so I needed to keep my distance.

We used to go to this Chinese joint—Robin loved their moo shu pork. I knew she'd appreciate it, so I ordered that and a couple of other dishes. The food broke the tension, but as much as I hated to, I knew I had to leave before the others did.

5

LUCA

HEADING BACK ON US 41, THE RADIO BARKED, SHOVING Robin's shapely image out of my head. Another code 38 in Golden Gate. A car was on the way, but the desk wasn't sure if this domestic disturbance involved a hostage situation and asked for any unit in the area to respond.

The Coastland Mall was in sight. I threw the strobe light on and hit the gas pedal. As I sped onto the overpass I saw a marked car, lights blazing, on Airport Pulling. He made up ground and was only a half mile behind me as I turned onto Coronado Parkway. By the time I made a right onto Tropical Way he was glued to my bumper.

I slid into a space behind two other marked cars in front of 16715 Tropical, which I quickly valued at well under three hundred K. As I hopped out I saw between houses the traffic whizzing by on Santa Barbara Boulevard. Two uniformed officers were straddling the front door, pleading with whoever was inside to open up.

"Yo, Luca."

I turned around. It was Bill Bailey.

"Dress rehearsal for the Indy Five Hundred?"

"I don't drive like no grandma when my fellow officers need me."

Bailey was a tad too enthusiastic of a brother in blue for me.

"Yeah, well, if you would've hit a bump, or a real grand-mother pulled onto the road, I'd be wondering what color suit to wear to your funeral."

A ruddy-faced officer who couldn't have been more than thirty had jogged over from the front door. I introduced myself as the young bucks fist-bumped.

"Reilly."

"What's the deal?"

Officer Reilly explained that someone he assumed was the husband answered the door and said he'd open the door but never did. Reilly asked to talk to the wife, who'd called 911, but the male claimed she was busy with the kids.

"This guy have a name?"

"Oh, sorry sir, Watkins, John. Caucasian, forty-two years of age."

"Employed?"

"Uh, don't know."

"Well find out. If this is a hostage situation we're gonna need as much data as possible." I headed to the door.

There were no sidelights to sneak a peek, so I rang the bell. Twenty seconds later I hit the door twice with the heel of my hand. A smoker's voice responded, "What do you want?"

"Just want to make sure everyone's all right."

"Everything's okay. There's no problem."

"I'm gonna need to see for myself."

"Why? I want my privacy."

"I understand, sir. However, it seems your wife called nine-one-one saying she felt threatened."

"That's bullshit."

I raised my voice a couple of notches. "I'm gonna ask one more time. Open the door, or I'll have it rammed open."

"Leave us alone."

I was about to threaten him when a sharp pain hit my abdomen. I hunched over for a second.

Reilly came up behind me. "You okay, Luca?"

"Yeah, got some gas pains. Gotta stay away from that Mexican food."

Reilly told me Watkins had just started a new job working nights at FedEx and asked if he should call for backup. I told him to hang on a minute and pounded the door again.

"I told you everything is okay, so leave us alone."

"Look, let's not make this into something you're going to regret. There's no reason to let FedEx know the cops are at your house, right?"

"Hey, don't play with my job, man. I need that."

"You're in control. You open, there's no reason to let FedEx know you had a spat with your woman."

The lock clicked and the door opened six inches. I wedged my foot in, nearly crushing Watkins' barefoot toes. Watkins was a skinny turd of a guy. Day-old stubble and what looked like a dove tattooed on his neck.

"See, there's nothing going on, so why don't you just leave us alone?"

"I'd like to see the missus."

"What for?"

"Well, she's the one who made the complaint."

He lowered his voice and opened the door another six inches. "She gets a little carried away from time to time. You know what I mean?"

As I said, "I sure do," I pulled the door open.

"Step outside, Mr. Watkins."

"This is my house. You can't force me out of my own damn house."

"Reilly, would you and Bailey arrest this gentleman for failing to obey a police order?"

"All right, all right. Can I put on shoes first?"

"Outside, Watkins. Now."

I stepped into the house and called out, "Mrs. Watkins? Detective Luca here. Can we have a word with you?"

The door to the bedroom slowly opened and a red-headed woman of about forty walked into the family room. She'd been crying. I followed her, thinking she probably made a great apple pie. Broken glass had been swept into a pile, and a broom rested against the couch.

"Are you okay?"

She nodded.

"How about the children?"

"They're both at school."

"What happened that made you call nine-one-one?"

"I shouldn't have called. It was a mistake. I don't want John to get in trouble. He didn't really do anything."

I rubbed my gut, man was it sore. "Take it easy. Let's see if we can settle this among ourselves. Okay?"

She brightened.

"It was really kinda nothing. John had gotten in from work at about five a.m. He needs to settle down. He can't go right to sleep, it's like his rhythm is off from working nights."

I nodded.

"He was watching TV, like he always does, but it was kinda loud, so I got up and asked him to lower it."

"Did he?"

She frowned. "He was being spiteful and raised it. So, I got a little bit mad. I didn't want the kids to wake up."

"What did you do?"

"I pulled the cable box plug out."

"And?"

"Well, he, you know, got upset. I shouldn't have done it. It takes too long for the cable to boot back up."

"Did he get physical with you?"

She looked at her feet. "No, not really."

"It's okay, you can tell me what happened. Nothing's gonna happen to John."

"It was nothing, really. He got up and plugged it back in, and I tried to unplug it, and we both went for the plug at the same time, you know, and we banged into each other and I lost my balance and banged into the table and the vase fell over." She gazed at the glass pile and teared up.

"It's okay. What happened next?"

She sniffled. "That vase was my mom's. She gave it to me. It's the only thing of hers I have. When it fell I got really mad, but it's all my fault."

"But when you called nine-one-one, you said you were threatened, afraid, for you and the kids."

"The kids got up and they, they were crying because we were arguing. So, I put them back to bed and stayed in my daughter's room till it was time for them to go to school."

"The kids went to school, then what?"

"Well, I was really angry about the vase, and he was sleeping, and I know it was stupid but I put the TV on real loud. It was stupid. I don't know why I did it. It was childish, but I wanted to get back at him."

"Go on."

"So, he woke up and started yelling. He was right, he needed his rest and all. I don't know what got into me, but I put the volume all the way up. He came flying out of the bedroom and he was cursing and chased me. I ran into the bathroom and he was banging on the door. I told him I was gonna call the police and he said to go ahead." She shrugged. "So, I did."

"Did he lay a hand on you?"

"No, no."

"The kids?"

"John would never do that."

"Did he push you into the table?"

"No, like I said, we both kinda collided."

"Do you want me to run him into the station, you know, to cool him off a bit?"

"No, he's cooled down. I mean he was mad I called, and he's right, it was stupid, but I didn't know what else to do."

"Nine-one-one is not a game, ma'am, but by all means, if you feel there's a danger to you or the children please don't hesitate to call."

She nodded.

"Stay here a minute. I'm gonna talk to your husband."

John Watkins had bummed a smoke from Bailey and was leaning on the entrance column.

"What do you say you open the garage?"

"Open the garage? What do you think you'll find there? Bodies?"

"Unless you want the neighbors to see you get in the back of a police car, I'd say we have a little talk out of their view."

Watkins punched in a code and the garage door lifted, revealing a lawn mower, an assortment of bicycles, and plastic kids' furniture.

"So why don't you tell me why the county's got three law enforcement officers here?"

His story didn't vary too much from his wife's, except when it came to the vase. He said he knocked into it by accident, but I knew he broke it on purpose. It was stupid and vengeful but a heck of a lot better than knocking your wife around.

"You know, John, I'm not one to be advising anyone on marriage, but one thing I can tell you is it ain't gonna get easier if you don't respect the things your wife holds dear to her. Wake up, you broke the only thing her mom left her."

"No, I didn't. It was an accident."

As I threw a palm up, my belly pain sharpened.

"Look, go in there and make up with your wife. Buy her something she likes to replace the vase. Surprise her with something."

He nodded like a bobblehead doll.

"Go ahead and make up before your kids get out of school."

"Thanks."

My pain receded, and as he headed for the door I said, "Hey, John, you like pie?"

"Uh, yeah, sure."

"What's your favorite?"

"I guess apple or blueberry."

"Does your wife bake?"

"Oh yeah, she's a great baker."

I smiled and left.

As I came up to Goodlette-Frank Road I remembered that Ron Vespo, one of the guys Phil's buddy Dom gave me, lived in Calusa Bay. I radioed in for the guy's telephone number and told Vespo I'd be dropping by.

Calusa Bay was a sky-blue collection of older coach homes in a primo location. Based on the location, I thought the units should trade for more than the two fifty to three hundred they were going for. I'd been thinking over the idea that it could be worth picking one up as an investment.

Vespo lived in a second-floor unit overlooking the clubhouse. I could hear kids playing Marco Polo in the pool as I hit the doorbell.

Glancing through the sidelight, I saw Vespo tucking his shirt in like a good boy as he approached.

Flashing my creds, I said, "Thanks for seeing me on short notice."

"No problem, Officer. Anything I can do to help Phil. This is scary, him just vanishing."

The apartment's furnishings were dated, and there were two credenzas crowded with sports trophies, mostly baseball.

"I understand Phil's done this before."

Vespo tilted his head as I clarified. "A couple of other contacts said Phil has taken off before, shacking up with a woman or two."

"Oh yeah, everyone knew he liked to screw around, but never for more than a couple of days, and he'd usually give some bullshit story to his wife."

"Robin?"

He smiled. "She's a piece of art, ain't she?"

I felt myself nodding and said, "So how long have you known Mr. Gabelli, and what's the nature of your relationship?"

Vespo told me he'd met Phil at the dog track in Bonita about seven or eight years ago through one Antonio Depas, who was a mutual friend. Vespo said Phil came to the track regularly, a lot of times with a different gal on his arm.

This was a side of Gabelli I hadn't heard. I dug in a bit. "What size wagers did Gabelli place?"

He shrugged. "No more than everyone else we hung with."

"What's a normal bet for your crowd?"

"I donno, about a hundred a race."

"That's a lot from where I come from. A guy could lose a grand in a day."

"Nah, you gotta hit something out of twelve races. Besides, we're pretty good at this."

Yeah, so good at gambling your couch is older than my grandmother, I thought.

"How often did Phil go to the track?"

"A couple of times a week."

"Sounds like a lot for a guy with a regular job."

Vespo shrugged. "He wouldn't be there all day. He would pop in, lay down some bets, and take off."

"He didn't watch?"

"Just one or maybe two."

"Sounds like he should've just called it in to his bookie."

Vespo's eyes narrowed but he remained silent. There was something there. I said, "Look, the last thing I wanna get involved with is chasing some bookie down. So, did Phil have a bookie?"

"He did, and a year maybe two years ago he got in a jam with him."

"Jam?"

"He had a bad streak of luck, that's all."

"Phil was making bets on the side and got in over his head?"

Vespo nodded.

"How did he climb out of the jam?"

"What do you think? His wife's loaded."

"Is there anything Phil's done that's unusual, you know, anything, like odd behavior or something secretive?"

"Nah, not really, he's pretty straight."

"You sure?"

"Yeah, the only thing that was weird, was like over a year ago. You see, when us guys are at the track we always check the racing form and we decide on how much we're betting and on what puppy. Then one of us goes to the window and buys all the tickets for everybody."

I nodded.

"Well, this one day, it was a Saturday, I remember because he was there the whole time. Anyway, he kept saying he had to go to the bathroom like almost before every race. So, we were ragging on him about his prostrate. Anyway, before one race he said he was going to take a leak and left. But when I went to get a brew, I saw him at one of the windows laying down more bets."

"Did you confront him?"

"It ain't my place. I'm not his father."

We talked some more but there was nothing else that stood out aside from Phil looking like he'd been bitten by the gambling bug. I got the name of the bookie these guys used, it was one I knew, along with the contact info for Antonio Depas before I got back in the car.

6

STEWART

"Achievement results from work realizing ambition. –
Adam Ant

THREE LONG, EXHAUSTING DAYS OF COMBING COLLIER AND
parts of Lee County helped to drain the emotion out of Robin.
It was sad, and I kinda felt bad she was so desperate, but she
needed the reality check. In another positive development,
her sister was finally getting out of Dodge. I knew getting
things back to normal, as quickly as possible, was the answer.

Two days later, the sheriff's office told Robin they were
following leads but offered zero evidence there was anything
strong. Though initially depressing for her, I thought it
helped. Things continued to settle down until Robin and her
preacher friend, who I think had eyes on her, organized a
night vigil.

I wasn't too happy about it, as she had moved from
distraught to regaining her footing somewhat. My concern,
besides the preacher man, was she'd get all emotional again
and take a step back. How could things ever get back to
normal if she was always a basket case?

It took me a good half hour before deciding on dark gray slacks and an off-white shirt. No rain was in the forecast, so it seemed safe to wear my new Gucci loafers. They were a splurge I couldn't afford, but they looked sweet.

The vigil was being held in Cambier Park, and it was way more crowded than I'd expected. Between the hundred or so candle holders and scores of curious tourists, the park was more than half full. Two weeks had zipped by since Phil had gone missing, so maybe people thought it was some kinda funeral.

The place looked spooky. The bandstand where Robin and preacher boy stood wasn't fully lit up. I skipped up the stairs to the stage as the pastor led the call for God's intervention and Phil's safe return. Good luck with all that. I stood off to the side and surveyed the crowd. All sorts of people were out there.

Scanning faces, I could only pick out a handful of familiar ones. I looked over at some morons who brought lawn chairs, like it was a concert or something, and spied Detective Luca leaning against a giant banyan tree.

What was he doing here? He had a cup of something in his hand and was staring at the stage as the praying dragged on. I'd bet the snake was probably trying to get close to Robin.

When the prayer was over, a singer I didn't know stepped up to the mic and begin leading the crowd through "He's Got the Whole World in His Hands."

I sang along and studied Luca, who wasn't singing. When his gaze began to move my way, I started crying. It wasn't a sobfest or nothing, just all of a sudden, I felt everything welling up. I moved toward Robin—I needed her, we needed each other.

A circle of people surrounded Robin, all of them in serious need of tissues. I couldn't get anywhere near her. Suddenly, preacher boy took the mic and led everyone in the Lord's Prayer. I'm no Holy Roller, but I can tell you the hairs on the back of my neck stood straight up. I looked by the banyan tree for Luca, but he wasn't there.

It must've been at least another fifteen minutes of singing and praying before Robin took the mic and thanked everyone for coming. Finally, it was over; that was something to thank God for. I was starving and hoped I could catch a bite alone with Robin. A ton of people surrounded her constantly. She needed some down time. We both needed it.

I broke into the huddle and pecked her cheek. I tried to fish for her hand but she pulled it away and said to the preacher, "Paul, this is Dom Stewart. He and Phil were, uh, are good friends."

"Nice to meet you, Reverend. What church are you with?"

He had real small hands, and I had to suppress a laugh as he blabbed about his church on Bonita Beach Road.

I tapped Robin on the shoulder. "What do you say we go out for some sushi? Just the two of us."

"Sushi sounds great, but what about everyone else?"

"What do you mean?"

"I can't just leave them. They came out for me, for Phil."

"Why not?"

She glared at me and I said, "Just kidding, lighten up."

To my chagrin, preacher boy suggested we go to Mel's Diner. I had no interest in going, other than to keep an eye on the preacher, but I went along, along with about ten more of us.

As I walked to the parking lot behind Fifth Avenue, I saw

Luca hanging around the back entrance to the Hob Nob. I didn't know what to do. Did he see me? It would look bad if I turned around, so I decided to keep walking. Just as I was crossing the street, a short-skirted blonde poked her head out of a door, and the detective followed her inside.

7

STEWART

"The best way to predict the future is to invent it." –
Alan Kay

ON THE WAY BACK HOME, NO MATTER HOW MANY TIMES I
changed the radio station, I kept thinking of Phil. After
spending time with Robin, I was usually floating, but now I
felt like crying again. No amount of blinking would erase the
image of his face that was burned in my mind. I was turning
into a frigging basket case, sucking my inhaler like a damn
lollipop. I bemoaned the fact that if only Phil would've taken
my advice we wouldn't be dealing with all this.

It was still vivid, after all this time. It wasn't an easy
subject to broach, but I'd set it up nicely, spending a lot of
energy debating the details of how, where, and when.

Phil, for all his faults, did a lot of volunteer work with
kids. Who knows why? Probably it was the guilt from
screwing around on Robin. Phil helped with the Boy Scouts,
with Big Brother, and went every Tuesday afternoon to the
Immokalee Child Care Center. The plan was to meet up at the

center, grab some dinner, and then we'd head over to the casino for a little blackjack and ladies action.

The smell of cumin and garlic was in the air as we settled into a green leather booth at Mi Ranchito. Knowing the menu, we ordered quickly. The waitress put down a bowl of chips and salsa and Phil started to go on about a new girl he'd met at work. And just like that I had my opening.

"Look, Philly, I don't want to talk out of school or anything, but what are you doing, man?"

Phil reached for a tortilla chip. "What are you talking about?"

"Come on, man, you're always screwing around."

He smiled. "Yeah, and what about it?"

"You got to stop it. It's not right, man. You're gonna get in trouble, I'm telling you."

He waved me off and dug a chip into the salsa. "I'm just having some fun, man. Nothing wrong with that. You always say you gotta seize the opportunities."

"But it's not fair to Robin."

"Don't you worry, I've got it handled all right with her."

"Yeah? You're treating her like a rag." I leaned in and lowered my voice. "She deserves better, man. Instead of running her through the mill, why don't you just leave her?"

Phil's eyes narrowed. "Who the hell you think you are? Stay the hell out of my business."

I froze. He'd never gotten pissed at me like that in the all the years we knew each other.

"I, uh, I'm just saying, it'd be best for all of us if, you know, if you just ended the marriage."

He put his hands on his hips. "All of us? Just what the hell does that mean?"

"Nothing, Philly, it doesn't mean anything. Look, just forget it, man. Sorry, I butted in."

Phil wagged his head and slid out of the booth.

"Where you going, Philly?"

It was a disaster, and our friendship never really recovered. I couldn't see where I'd gone wrong. It made sense to me. He was a terrible husband and was always playing with other women, even though they couldn't shine a light on Robin. It didn't make sense, and things got worse.

Not only was he pissed, but he piled on by telling Robin, setting her on a warpath with me. I didn't understand why Robin couldn't see that I was looking out for her. She was angry as all hell and accused me of trying to break up her marriage. Here I thought I had a grand plan to make everyone happy, and it blew up in my face.

After that episode, even though she caught him screwing around a bunch of times, it never seemed as good as it once was between us. I was baffled.

Lately we hadn't seen each other as much, and I thought that would get a lot better with Phil gone, but it didn't. A void separated us, which I'd have to work on. Things were messy now, but I knew it would work out. I pulled up to my house, reminding myself to call Detective Luca in the morning. There was something I wanted to tell him.

8

LUCA

STEWART WAS EITHER SMARTER THAN HE SEEMED, OR HE thought he was smarter than he was. Things were just off. Whether they were off by a smidge or a country mile was the question.

When I asked him why he never mentioned that Phil liked to gamble, he said he didn't think it was important. Then when I said he could've gotten in over his head and in deep trouble, Stewart said no way. They had plenty of money, and if he lost big it was no big deal.

He seemed to be covering up his friend's gambling escapades. According to Vespo, his buddy Phil was at the track a couple of times a week, and Stewart never mentions it? Stewart just said every now and then they'd go to the Immokalee casino, but he said Phil never laid any big bets and was more interested in the cocktail waitresses than the gaming tables.

It didn't add up, and now the question was if this meant something or not. If Phil got in trouble by gambling I didn't see why Stewart would cover it up. Was I missing something?

Or was Stewart being cute? Hiding an important fact he

knew we'd be interested in, would serve him how? It just didn't make sense.

I was hoping Phil's bookie would provide some clarity to the mud bowl on my desk as I picked up a criminal record.

Looking through Butch Turnberry's file, it seemed like he was nothing more than a bully whose best days were back in high school. A jock who excelled at football, Turnberry had bounced from job to job after graduating and picked up a handful of assaults along the way.

Stewart had given me his name, but I couldn't see a small-time thug crossing over to something more sinister. With Vargas on vacation, I had to prioritize. Could I put Turnberry on ice? I was on the fence because one of the assaults involved a bat. It wasn't considered a deadly weapon, but I'd seen my share of bashed skulls up in New Jersey.

Staring at Turnberry's mug shot, I begged it to talk to me. Nothing.

Grabbing a bottle of Tums out of my drawer, I spilled three out and chewed the chalky tablets as I thought. Gabelli's place of work still needed a visit, but looking at the thug's picture again, I decided that would have to wait until I saw this thug.

TURNBERRY LIVED in an area known as Naples Park. To me, the area was the ultimate real estate enigma. Nestled off Vanderbilt Beach Road, west of 41, Naples Park had a salad bowl of homes. The location was a ten, but there was an epidemic of bungalows with so many cars parked in front they looked like used car lots.

There were stretches of streets where homes had been totally redone, but they could be next to an unkempt shack.

I'd always thought the area had promise and wanted to invest in it. I thought it could be the next Park Shore but was cautioned by a realtor friend to stay away.

As I suspected, Turnberry lived in a putrid-blue shelter with eight cars scattered on the grass. Two of them were on blocks, and another had a tarp over it. Pitying the people living in the manicured house to the left, I walked to the door.

A shirtless teenager came to the door and sneered when I flashed my credentials asking for Turnberry. He turned his back on me and shouted for my target as he disappeared.

Six foot and broad shouldered, Turnberry was a V-shaped slab of granite with just a hint of a beer belly. I held up my badge as he approached. He eyed me suspiciously and didn't open the screen door.

"What do you want?"

"You know a guy named Phil Gabelli?"

"Who?"

I'd been doing this so long I knew the first questions always resulted in denials. I held a picture to the screen. "Be easier to see without the screen in the way."

The door creaked open, revealing a pair of sneakers that had their own zip code and a squiggly scar on a knee. He leaned toward the picture and shook his head.

"No idea who you're talking about."

That was denial two. There's usually three or four before the, *oh yeah, I remember*.

"How about Dom Stewart? You know him?"

I could see the calculation he was making. He'd been around the block. It was a bit of a dance sometimes.

"Name sounds a little familiar, but what's this all about?"

"Dom and Phil are best friends."

"Congratulations."

"Stewart said you knew Gabelli."

"Who the hell can remember everybody they've met?"

Right on schedule, a criminal clam began to open.

"Stewart said he played football with you. Was on your team."

"Bullshit. He never played. You see, on a field you never know what's gonna happen after the coin flip. Stewart couldn't handle stuff like that, he had to have an angle."

I knew he didn't play with Turnberry, but the angle thing was new.

"What do you mean about looking for an angle?"

"Come on, man, you know what I mean. Those guys that don't like to play fair and square."

An ethics lesson from a thug? This was a first for me. I tucked the data away and got back to the business at hand.

"I know what you're saying about Stewart. Anyway, he said you knew Gabelli." I offered the picture again and the amnesia receded.

"Yeah, I've seen him around with Stewart."

"Where?"

"Down at the casino."

"You gamble much?"

He shook his head. "Only suckers gamble."

You had to admire this guy. Been in jail, lived in a rat hole, but he was a fountain of wisdom. Maybe the philosophy department at Gulf Coast University could use him.

"They were gambling then?"

"Some gambling, drinking, and checking the ladies out. Just a guys' night out."

"Either one of them ever ask for a loan?"

He laughed. "You're coming to the wrong place if you're looking for money. I never lend money out. It always gets you in trouble, trust me."

Another piece of advice from the sage of life.

"I hear you didn't get along with Gabelli. What was the beef about?"

"Beef? Who said that?"

"Your buddy Stewart."

"He ain't no buddy of mine, just a guy I know."

"Well, this guy you know, he said to check with you on what happened to Phil Gabelli."

"What do you mean, what happened? What the hell is that supposed to mean?"

"Said you didn't like Gabelli, and, who knows, you've been known to assault people. Who knows, maybe you threw him a beating."

He took the tiniest step forward, and I leaned toward him as a warning.

"I don't know what bullshit you're chasing down, mister. But I don't know what you're talking about. This Gabelli dude, he had a smart mouth, he thought who the hell he was."

"You had to put him in his place?"

"I never laid a finger on him. Would've loved to knock him off his high horse, but I'm practicing restraint these days. Even been meditating."

Meditating. I'd pay to see this hood humming, cross-legged on the floor.

"Guess you have to find a new chant. Weren't you picked up in a brawl at Rusty's about ten days ago?"

"Look, that wasn't my fault. That punk was egging me on. Kept moving the cue ball. I told him to cut it out, but he didn't listen. I had to do something; everybody was watching. I got a reputation, you know, I gotta keep it intact."

Wow, he wasn't looking to be the Dalai Lama after all.

"Did Gabelli egg you on?"

"You got it all wrong, man."

"Do I?"

"Let me tell you, he was a wiseass, no doubt, but he didn't threaten me or screw me around like that asshole in Rusty's. Closest he came was when he kept pestering me, wanting to bet me he could pick up this woman at a blackjack table."

Woman and Phil Gabelli, perfect together. "Did you bet him?"

"I told you I don't gamble. Besides, I hate to say it, but he did have a way with women."

"So, I hear."

Turnberry was a dead end, I was beginning to realize. I'd poke around a bit more, but the question circling around my head was why Stewart fingered him as someone to talk to.

"You get along with Stewart?"

"Look, I didn't touch either one of those guys."

"I'm not saying you did. Just trying to understand what I'm doing here talking to you."

"You'll have to ask Stewart."

Finally, a piece of advice I could use.

9

STEWART

"Success each day should be judged by the seeds sown, not the harvest reaped." - John C. Maxwell

I SAID, "HELLO, DETECTIVE LUCA?"

"Yes, sir. Who's this?"

"Dom Stewart, you know, Robin and, uh, Phil's friend."

"What can I do for you?"

Not even a freaking hello?

"Well, I got to thinking about Phil and his wandering eye and I remembered that there was this girl from the islands he was tied up with."

"Islands?"

"Yeah, I think it was Martinique, or maybe St. Maarten, one of those French islands in the Caribbean."

"Go on."

"You know, I'm ninety-nine percent sure it was Martinique. Well, Phil was into her for a while, I mean he was really into her, big time. He'd see her a lot and they'd disappear for days at a time."

"When was this?"

"About three years ago."

"He'd go down to Martinique to see her?"

"Sometimes, but she'd come up a lot. She worked for an airline. I think it was American."

"What's her name?"

"Not certain, her first name was Nicole, though. Last name was something like Paster, Passor . . ."

"This was three years ago, you say?"

"Maybe a bit longer."

"And then it ended after how long?"

"I don't know exactly, but I'd say the better part of a year."

"And do you know if they picked up again?"

I had to admit that was a good question I hadn't thought of.

"Not that I know of."

"Okay, we'll look into it, but it sounds like a long shot."

"No, you gotta check it out, Detective."

"Why's that?"

"He and her had a kid together."

"A kid?"

"Yeah, a little boy."

"Does Robin know about this?"

Again, calling her Robin. "No, Robin would've killed him. Robin wanted kids like crazy, but Phil didn't, said it'd cramp his lifestyle. I even think, but I'm not one hundred percent, that he made her have an abortion."

"Robin?"

"Yeah, it's really sad. She just wants to be a mother. Every woman should be able to."

"Do you think Robin found out somehow and killed Phil in a rage?"

"I donno. I don't think so, but I guess you never know, do you?"

"I don't understand something, Mr. Stewart."

Mr. Stewart? "What's that, Detective?"

"You just remembered this relationship?"

"Yeah, Philly had a lot of horses in his stable."

"Any of them had kids with him?"

"Uh, no."

"Any of them from an island?"

"No."

"Seems like most people would remember those things, Mr. Stewart."

Shit, I shouldn't have laid it on so thick. I wanted to hang up.

"I guess I just didn't think he'd go back to her."

"I see. By the way, I went to see Turnberry, and he said he had no idea why you gave his name to me. Said he hardly knew you guys."

"That's a bunch of bull. We knew him from school."

"But you and Phil didn't see him much these days, right?"

"Here and there. He's been arrested a bunch of times, went to jail. I thought it was someone you should check out, that's all. I'm just trying to help."

"Okay, Mr. Stewart. We'll look into what you've told us."

10

LUCA

THE MORE I TALKED WITH STEWART THE MORE UNEASY I became. Something was off with him. I couldn't put my finger on it and had chalked it up to him being a kinda oddball, but now he comes to me about some long-term relationship with an island girl Phil had a kid with? And after the goose chase with Turnberry?

He should've spilled the beans on day one. This was important. Another sharp pain hit my abdomen, almost taking my breath away. This was going on too long. I needed to have a doctor check it out. As it subsided I started to think maybe Stewart was just protecting his buddy and didn't want Robin to know. Stewart was certainly protective of her, a little too much, if you asked me.

Man, what an embarrassment it would be if all this time Phil was sitting on a beach with his island family while Robin was organizing search parties. It'd be the top news story for weeks.

I missed not being able to kick this case around with my old partner, J. J. Cremora. We'd bounce more things off each other than a racquetball court. He was a good cop and kept me from being anal, most of the time. I still couldn't believe he was gone. Losing him was the toughest thing I've gone through. The divorce was nothing compared to him dying. Only consolation was his passing got me down to Naples.

We'd been through so much together, I swear if it wasn't for him I'd never have bounced back from the Barrow case. A picture of the kid hanging from the pipes in his cell rushed back into my head.

I stood up. The sun was shining through the windows, but the room was closing in on me. I headed to the bathroom to splash cold water on my face. No matter how many times I told my reflection to shake the blue feeling, it didn't work. I needed a dose of Southwest Florida's elixir, and since it was almost lunch time, I headed straight for the Turtle Club to get it.

It wasn't quite noon, but the restaurant's beach deck was nearly full. I snagged a table and was mesmerized by the placid gulf until a woman in a cover-up was shown to the table next to me. She was a knockout, and I said, "Beautiful day."

She smiled. "It's been nice the whole week."

"I know what you mean. We don't even need a weather channel down here."

"You live here?"

"Yep, I'm stuck in paradise."

"It must be nice."

I nodded. "Where you from?"

Her name was Kayla and she was in from Chicago to attend a marketing workshop. As far as I was concerned she didn't need any help selling; I'd buy anything she was hawking. The workshop had ended and this gem was enjoying a few days of vacation she'd tacked onto the trip.

She said, "This is my first time at the Turtle Club. I tried to come yesterday but it was packed."

"What do you say we help them out? I can move over to your table and open up a table for some lucky souls."

She agreed and I smiled at the thought that my buddy JJ had come through for me again.

BACK FROM LUNCH, I logged onto the international portal and filled out two requests with Interpol, one for each of this island girl's possible last names. It usually took three to four days for a response to come in from the Europeans, but who knew how long or even if they followed things up in the Caribbean?

Calling American Airlines headquarters in Fort Worth, I was greeted by a voice-mail maze. By the third menu I was lost and had to call back.

The woman in human resources was nice enough but said that the airline considered employee files to be confidential. I explained it was a police matter and only wanted to know if a certain person worked for them and how to contact her.

She put me on hold for a minute before telling me I had to put the request in writing. Asking how long it would take after they received my request, I got some corporate mumbo jumbo about clearing it through their legal and human resources departments.

I pumped out the request and started thinking about the date I'd made with Kayla when my phone rang, delivering an unexpected nugget that complicated the Phil Gabelli case.

11

STEWART

"The gem cannot be polished without friction nor man without trials." - Confucius

THREE DAYS AFTER I HAD TOLD LUCA ABOUT PHIL'S OLD Caribbean cutie, the detective called and asked me to come to his office. I was sure he'd found someone that would fit my island girl and picked out a nice pair of white slacks for the occasion. Excited but dreading the drive through traffic to get to the municipal complex, I ran the electric shaver over my face and changed my shirt before hopping in the car.

I pulled off Tamiami Trail and into a space in the garage. It wasn't hot, and the humidity was low, but my shirt was darkening as I emptied my pockets for the security check.

Luca came out before I could read a page of *Men's Health*. He wasn't friendly, and my guard was even higher as he showed me into his cramped office. Luca's desk and credenza were piled with files, but there wasn't a picture of any family or friends.

"Have a seat. You want something to drink?"

That was better.

"Nah, I'm okay, thanks. What did you want to see me about? You have a lead on Phil?"

"No, but when we do it'll be Robin who'll be informed."

Robin. Like they were old friends. I had a feeling from the get-go this slickster would try to make a move on her. I wondered what she thought of him. Of all the detectives in the world I had to get the one who looked like George Clooney. No doubt, he was frigging handsome. I'd just have to confront Robin and ask her what she thought of him.

Luca leaned forward and said, "How come you never told me you and Mrs. Gabelli had an affair?"

Whoa. Who the hell told him that? Couldn't have been Robin? No way. My chest was tightening when I said, "It's got nothing to do with anything."

"In my book, it certainly does."

"How'd you find out?"

"Never mind the how. I want to know what that was all about."

I dug out my inhaler.

"It's none of your business. Shit, you go around probing into people's private lives? That's bullshit, you ask me."

"Noted. Now, your friend is missing, and you were sleeping with his wife. Sounds pretty coincidental, wouldn't you agree?"

"So, what now, I'm a suspect?"

"We look at everyone, especially those close to him. Your, shall we say, relationship with his wife is an interesting element."

"Well, I had nothing to do with what happened to Phil."

Luca leaned back. "Just what happened to him?"

"I don't know. He went missing, that's all."

Luca grimaced and rubbed his side. "You sure of that?"

What the hell did he mean by that?

"Look, I told you, Phil liked going around screwing every tail he could get his hands on. He's probably getting laid right now."

Luca leaned back and put his foot on a corner of his desk.

"You want to know something else interesting?"

I didn't like the sound of that so I just shrugged.

"Seems you told Robin to leave Phil. Is that true?"

How the hell did he know that? I mean, Robin, for God's sake, what are you doing here?

"Look, like I told you, Phil was always cheating on Robin. It was an abusive relationship. She was being made out to be a damn fool for Chrissake!"

"You a marriage counselor now?"

"Hey, me and Robin are good friends."

"Friends? I'd say it was a lot more than that."

"What are you getting at? You got something on me more than an old affair?"

Luca cocked his head and smiled. He was one smug bastard.

I said, "Don't forget, Mr. Detective, that this was a couple of years ago."

Luca suddenly grabbed his stomach and gritted his teeth. Then he doubled over for a second. He didn't look like he was feeling too good, so I stood.

"If you don't have anything else, I'm going."

12

LUCA

THE PAIN LASTED LONGER THAN USUAL. I SHOULDN'T HAVE let Stewart leave, but it felt like it was never going to go away. Stewart was a snake. He was screwing his best friend's wife. How damn low can you go?

At least he didn't compound it by lying. Boy, I would have loved to have nailed him on that. Stewart should have said something to us about the affair. For that matter, Robin should have too. People think they can keep these dark secrets between themselves, but if you ask me, the only way two people can keep a secret is when one of them is dead.

The affair was a potential bombshell. It opened up all kinds of possibilities. Stewart could've done away with his buddy to get another chance with Robin, or both of them could be playing star roles in a conspiracy to do in Phil. Even Robin, though I couldn't see it, could've done it alone. Everything was open now that I knew she wasn't the faithful wife she painted herself to be.

I made a mental note to check if there were any insurance policies that Robin could benefit from as I headed for the bathroom.

A touch of red in my urine alarmed me. No more waiting; if I couldn't get an appointment with my doctor for tomorrow, I'd go to the walk-in place on Vanderbilt. I gave a passing thought to heading over to the urgent care clinic right then, but I didn't want anything to stand in the way of the date I had with Kayla.

Though I totally missed my old partner JJ, working alone seemed to suit me most times. But with a case that seemed to grow hair every day, I looked forward to Mary Ann coming back from vacation. She was my first female partner, and though she gave me a hard time every now and then and was into astrology, she was as good as they come. Plus, there was something about her I couldn't put my finger on. Sometimes she just looked sugar sweet and other times as plain as white bread. Either way, I was staying away, or at least hoped I would.

Tomorrow we'd divvy up the chores. I'd follow up on the affair with Robin and dig deeper into Stewart, maybe even pay a visit to his workplace. Meanwhile, Mary Ann would hunt down the bookie Phil had been indebted to and find out what she could about Robin and Phil's finances.

My cell sounded off a reminder I was due in court at two o'clock. Thank God for the reminder. I had forgotten about having to testify in a car theft ring case. An offshoot of the Russian mob had settled in Miami and had profited from a pretty clever scheme. The Russians partnered with a group of Haitian criminals in Collier County who would steal specific high-end cars requested by the Russians.

Naples had a ton of rich cats with expensive cars they hardly drove. Many of the owners were away for weeks at a time, and the Russians had a ton of intelligence on the who, when, and where. The Haitians would grab the cars and run them over to Miami in trailers marked with the FedEx brand.

Once they arrived, the Russians would load them into containers and ship them to Eastern Europe. Most of the cars were out of the country before they were reported stolen. It was a perfect scheme until they got greedy and started to grab cars whose owners knew they'd gone missing and reported them stolen.

The Russians used duplicate vehicle identity numbers to get the hot cars through export control, mirroring the same scheme they used with selling actual social security numbers to illegals. It was such a simple idea in a world so complicated that it flew under the radar for way too long.

I smiled heading to court, thinking all good things gotta come to an end.

RELIEF SPILLED over when I saw Kayla waiting at Baleen. She looked as good, no, make that better, than the first time I saw her. I'd upgraded quite a few ladies over the years, always induced by the haze of alcohol, but this gal was the real deal. Kayla was dressed to kill. Boy, was I glad I had showered and changed.

I liked that she wasn't at the bar but was standing in La Playa's lobby. Despite the open way we met, she clearly wasn't comfortable being alone at a strange bar.

She pecked my cheek hello and we headed through a throng of people there to see the sunset. I worried that there wouldn't be a good table to watch the sun sink into the gulf, but my buddy at the bar had done his part for me.

We settled into a table on the terrace and I ordered a bottle of Viognier. I couldn't resist ordering a little-known varietal to impress her.

"Wow, you must have some connections. Look at this. It's beautiful out here."

"One of the perks of living here."

"Well, it was sweet of you to bring me here. It's a really nice place."

"It's my pleasure. You deserve it."

I think she actually blushed. This gal might be too good to be true.

"So how was your day today? Catch any crooks?"

"Thankfully, there's not as much crime down here as up in Jersey. But today I spent, or should I say wasted, most of the day in court."

"What happened?"

"I was supposed to testify in a high-end car theft ring that we broke up, but the judge adjourned the trial."

"So, they got off?"

"No, no. An adjournment is like a time-out. The defense lawyers made a series of motions, every one of them baseless in my opinion, preventing me from getting on the stand. It was just another waste of time in a system bogged down by too much legal maneuvering."

"Sorry. That must be frustrating."

She understood? What did I do to deserve this?

I nodded. "Sometimes, but anyway, what were you up to today?"

She began telling me she went to a beach downtown to check out the Old Naples feel when the stabbing feeling in my gut began again. I excused myself to go hit the men's room, feeling like I was gonna wet my drawers.

Pushing through the door, I felt lightheaded and bumped into a guy helping a kid wash up at the sink. I hit the urinal afraid to look down, and when I did it was a sea of red.

"Shit!"

"Hey, buddy, take it easy with the language."

"I, I . . ."

The room began to spin and my knees buckled.

13

LUCA

I CAME TO IN THE EMERGENCY ROOM AT NCH AND DIDN'T know what was worse, the stabbing in my gut or the pounding headache that blurred my vision. A forest of poles held bags leading to each of my arms. As I struggled to remember, a pair of white coats entered the cubicle I was calling home.

"Mr. Luca, I'm Dr. Mancino, and this is Nurse Mary."

I nodded. "What happened to me?"

"You're bleeding internally. The blood loss caused your hemoglobin count to drop, causing you to lose consciousness."

"Bleeding?"

"We discovered a couple of tumors in your bladder that are hemorrhaging."

Oh, no, tumors? Please don't tell me it's cancer.

"We're administering a drug to stem the bleeding, but we'll have to do further testing and grab a biopsy."

I heard myself ask, "Do I have cancer?"

"We're going to do a full assessment before we make any prognostications."

"I know it's early, but based on your experience, Doc, what do you think?"

"It's likely cancer, but even if it is, it appears not to have breached the bladder's wall. So, don't get overly concerned at this point."

"Don't get concerned? You tell me I have cancer, and I'm pissing blood, for Chrissakes."

"I understand, Mr. Luca. It's quite natural to be alarmed, but the medicine you're receiving will get the bleeding under control. Now, before we go, do you have any other questions?"

Instead of asking how long do I got? I said, "My head hurts like hell."

"I'm sure it does. You apparently hit your head when you lost consciousness. It's nothing serious. It will dissipate in a day or so. I'll order you an IV bolus dose of Tylenol that'll help."

In the morning, an oncologist named Murray came to see me right before I was wheeled into an operating room. They were going to do a biopsy to get more information on my tumors. It was scary as all hell, but Dr. Murray assured me that the scans showed the tumors were something that could be removed in surgery. He said I'd be good as new in a couple of months.

Before they put me out, I got to thinking that besides my headache, which had gotten a wee bit better, the pain in my abdomen had disappeared, but just lying there made me angry. How the fuck did this happen? I was too young for this. In a little while they were going to start the first procedure, then I'd have surgery, and who knows what after that. Things had been going too well, I guess. Knowing I'd now have to go through hell didn't feel good. I was scared and hoped like mad Murray was right when he said I'd be okay.

MY PARTNER VARGAS had heard what happened and called me for the second time from some Caribbean island. After I hung up, a couple of guys from the precinct came by to see me. Still under the influence of anesthesia, I was nodding off while they stood around in the room. Not in the mood for any damn company, I didn't try to keep it a secret. I dozed off, and when I woke they were gone. I turned my attention to the boob tube like it was something by Michelangelo.

Even though I was groggy, I could sense the appearance of Dr. Murray with yet another white coat, which was not a good sign.

"How are you feeling, Mr. Luca?"

"I guess as good as I can, considering my situation. How did everything go?"

The doctors exchanged glances and Murray said, "This is Dr. Lino. He's a reconstruction surgeon."

Nodding slowly, I tossed around the word reconstruction.

Dr. Lino said, "Mr. Luca, things are more complicated than originally thought. Though the biopsy evidenced a not particularly aggressive form of cancer, the additional scans we ran show evidence the tumors have breached the bladder's wall."

I looked at Dr. Murray, who'd pulled his lips in.

"What does all this mean, Doc?"

Dr. Murray said, "Considering the breach, we have to be super cautious to ensure the cancer does not spread. I'm afraid we'll have to remove your bladder."

Could I survive without a bladder? I guess so, if they're talking about taking it out. How would I piss? My mind was off to the races.

"Mr. Luca?"

"I'm sorry, I just can't process all this."

"We know it's a lot to think about. It's completely normal."

"What's going to happen to me? Am I gonna make it?"

"Yes, yes. As long as the cancer has not spread, and there's absolutely no evidence to believe it has, you'll be fine."

This was the same guy who originally said it hadn't breached the wall, so I took zero comfort in what he spit out.

"You said you'd have to take out my bladder. Don't I need one? How am I going to live without a bladder?"

"Well, there are a couple of options." Murray turned to Lino.

"Optimally, we'd be able to craft a de facto bladder for you out of your large intestine. We'd section off a piece and redirect the urinary tract."

That sounded like I'd be pretty normal.

"What's the downside, Doc?"

"Not much, as long as we can do it. The only thing is, you'll lose the nerve endings that alert you to relieve yourself. In other words, you won't experience the urge to go."

"You mean I'll have to wear a frigging diaper?"

"No, no. We recommend you adhere to a schedule of relieving yourself every two hours or so."

I exhaled. "Okay, okay. I can do that."

"One other thing is, you'll have to sit on the bowl and kinda force the urine out."

So, I had to sit like a girl, okay, I can handle that, still miles better than wearing Depends.

"Of course, there's no guarantee we'll be able to construct a bladder. If we're not able to do it, the other options are to build an internal reservoir that you'd have to pump out."

"What? How would it get the piss out?"

"You'd have an opening. It'd be capped, and you'd insert a tube to remove the fluids."

I shook my head. "That's crazy."

"Alternatively, we could have an external vessel collect the urine and you would dump its contents out."

A bag of piss hanging off me. That'd go real nice with the ladies. I was finished. They kept talking and I kept sinking. I heard them say goodbye and was left to ruminate whether I'd just gotten on an endless treadmill of doctor visits.

14

STEWART

"All our dreams can come true, if we have the courage to pursue them." - Walt Disney

"OH, WE CAN BEAT THEM. THEN WE CAN BE HEROES, IF ONLY for a day. We can be heroes." I loved singing this Bowie tune. It's my all-time favorite song. It says it all. Man, it made me feel good hearing it as I drove on 75.

Luca hadn't barked up my tree for a few days now. He must have dug into the affair with Robin and hadn't found anything he could run with. Even though he was leaving me alone, I just couldn't shake the feeling he was gonna show up with some Colombo crap.

The traffic on 75 was thick and slow going. Man, was I sick of driving to North Ft. Myers every day. What made it worse was that it was for a job I hated. No way was I doing this much longer. Life's way too short, and pretty soon I'd be forty, and then fifty, and well, who knows what will happen? Life moves at the speed of light, and it'll be over before you know it. Why did most people just trudge along like zombies?

Not me, I'd trade an hour in the sunshine for ten years in some dreary place.

Maybe Robin would be up to a nice vacation when things settled down and we'd reconnect. We were alike; she'd shake this nightmare and realize she'd have to move on. We used to always talk that the only way to live was to enjoy when and where you could. Things change in the blink of an eye; now she knew it better than anybody. I was betting she'd come to her senses soon.

Robin liked to spend money, not waste it, but enjoy it. She liked to say, save something, but don't deprive yourself of what you wanted now, as you don't know if you'll even be here later. She was right. Damn right. No question in my mind, it's miles better to live a couple of great years than thirty shitty years of scraping by. I'll worry about the future when and if it ever gets here.

It was already past nine and I was late again. I'd have to catch more bullshit from Greely, I thought, as a state trooper came flying up the median.

Grabbing my phone, I pressed Robin's number.

"Hey, Robin. How you doing?"

"Okay. What's the matter?"

"Nothing, everything's good. Just checking in on my way to work."

"Oh, thanks."

I asked, "What are you doing today?"

"I don't know. I was actually thinking of taking a ride into the office."

That's my girl, I thought, but said, "You sure? It's a good idea and all, but."

"I can't hang around here anymore. It's just too depressing."

"It'll get better as time passes. You'll see."

"I don't know, Dom. I don't know about anything."

"You've got to take your time. Everything's gonna work out. Life just moves on, like an escalator, whether you're on it or not." I cringed, escalator, did I really say that?

"I don't know what I'm gonna do without him."

"It's tough, I know, but don't give up hope."

"Thanks, but I keep thinking there's no use hoping he'll show up."

"You never know. There's been a lot of strange cases, and this could be one of them."

"I hope you're right."

"Look, why don't you go to the office. It'll keep your mind busy."

"You're right. I think I will. Have a good day."

"Oh, Robin, have you heard from that detective, Luca?"

"Not for a few days. That's what I think has got me down."

And me up, I thought.

"I'm sure they're on the case."

"I don't know, I'm losing faith in them."

"You're just depressed. You need to get away for a while. Take a break."

"I don't know about that."

"It'll be good for you. Maybe we could go together."

"It doesn't sound right."

I was still on 75 but said, "Just think it over. Hey, look, I'm sorry, but I just pulled up to the office. I'll talk to you later."

15

LUCA

TODAY WAS THE DAY. THOUGH THEY GAVE ME TIME TO THINK it over, I wanted the cancer out of me before it spread. It was only five days since I'd collapsed, but the surgery was gonna happen today.

Around noon they were going to take me downstairs to the OR. My chest began to tighten as I rolled around whether or not to get a second opinion. The doctors seemed to know what they were doing, and they said they had done this procedure almost a hundred times. That was ton of experience in my book. Then the thought hit me: I didn't know if they were all done here, at NCH. I should've asked about that. Shouldn't I? If someone from the hospital screwed up it could be the end of me.

It was difficult not to feel foolish. I'd always pontificated that we had to get comfortable with our own mortality and that our culture lived in denial, but since my diagnosis, I hadn't slept without narcotics. I just couldn't help it. It was irrational and counter to the way I lived. People always loved to talk about what happened to someone else, and I knew it wasn't *if* something was going to happen to you but a matter of *when*.

It was the truest statement ever expressed, but now, facing the when part, I couldn't stop feeling like I'd been robbed blind. I continued to wallow in my sorrow for another ten minutes until a cute nurse broke the funk up. After she left, I did a reasonable job of convincing myself everything would work out.

The door swung open and my partner appeared, holding a teddy bear balloon. A shiver ran down my neck. What was she doing here? Vargas wasn't due back for two more days. Oh no, if she came back early, she must know something.

"Vargas, you finally off vacation?"

"Hi, Frankie. How you feeling?"

"I'm all right."

"You sure?"

"Yeah. Why, I don't look good?"

"I see your vanity is intact." She put the balloon on the nightstand.

"Very funny."

"Seriously, Frank, what's going on? I'm really worried about you."

I exhaled. "Cancer of the bladder."

The color drained out of Vargas's face and she put her hand on the nightstand. "Oh my God."

"Don't get crazy. I'll survive it."

"But how? I mean, just like that?"

"Who knows? I had some blood in my pee-pee the last couple of days and some stomach pain, but that was it."

"I remember you saying your stomach hurt weeks ago. I told you at least five times to go to the doctor."

"It wouldn't have changed anything, Mommy."

"What are they gonna do? Chemo?"

I shook my head. "Surgery. In a couple of hours."

Vargas leaned against the bed. "Today?"

She really gave a damn. My throat was closing, and all I could do was nod.

"What do the doctors say?"

"They're going to remove the tumors and some of the bladder, but they'll have to see when they get in there."

"I'm so sorry, Frank." Vargas patted my hand.

I swallowed. "Don't worry, I'll be okay."

"I'm praying for you, Frank. I said at least a hundred Hail Mary's on the flight."

She was so sincere I almost started bawling, but I eked out a thank you.

"After the surgery, what's the recovery time?"

"They didn't really say." And I never really asked. "But a couple of months, I guess, till I'm back torturing your Latin tail."

She smiled. "Can't wait."

"What's going on at the job?"

"Not much, same old same old."

"Anything on the Gabelli case?"

"Come on, Frank, you've got to concentrate on taking care of yourself."

"You know, there's something about that Stewart guy that don't sit right with me."

"But they're buddies."

"Some buddy, Stewart was in the sack with his pal's wife."

"That was a couple years ago. Gabelli has a history of taking off. Maybe this time he's just not coming back."

"What did you find out about his bookie?"

"Couldn't get near Tommy Serra. I'm waiting on a contact to get me in."

"Be careful with those guys. You know why they call him Tommy Thumbs?"

Vargas shrugged.

"When Tommy was coming up, he was an enforcer for the Bigiottis, and when somebody didn't pay, he'd smash their thumbs with a hammer."

"Nice, real nice. You think the guy's the type to knock off a debtor?"

"I don't see it. No sense killing someone who owes you. You'd never collect that way. But you never know, something could've gotten out of hand."

"Or they needed to make an example out of someone."

"Now you're thinking, Vargas. That vacation was good for you. Hey, if you get a chance, check out where Stewart works. You never know what we'll learn."

A pair of nurses came in to prep me for the surgery and Vargas put a rosary in my hand. I valiantly tried to blink away the tears as she said goodbye.

16

STEWART

"Some make it happen, some watch it happen, and some say, 'What happened?'" - Anonymous

MY CELL RANG. IT WAS HER. SWEET.

"Hey, Robin. What's shaking, sunshine?"

"I called for Detective Luca, but he's out on sick leave."

I pumped a fist in the air. "Oh. I wonder what happened to him."

"Now nobody is going to be looking for Phil."

Here we go again. Sometimes she could be so dramatic. "I'm sure they work in teams. Don't panic, Robin."

"I'm not panicking, Dom! Every day Phil is gone it's more likely he'll never come back. I can feel it, that something happened to him, and you don't seem to care."

"I care. He was my best friend."

"Well, you're not doing much to help him."

"That's not fair, Robin. Look, I know it's not looking good, but you never know. He could be kidnapped or something by some lunatics."

"Something bad has happened to him. I had a very bad dream last night."

So that was it, a dream unsettled her. I calmed her down and told her I'd contact the police and find out who was taking over the case from Luca.

My call for Luca was connected to a woman by the name of Mary Ann Vargas. She sounded nice over the phone. I wondered what she looked like.

"I was looking for Detective Luca."

"He's out on leave. I'm his partner. What can I do for you?"

"Oh, I hope he's okay."

"He'll be fine."

"Good, you see, he was handling a missing person case, and we're wondering what's going on with it."

"Who is the person in question?"

"You have more than one?"

"Name?"

She was another pile of fun.

"Gabelli, Phil Gabelli. You know anything about it?"

"Of course. As I said, I'm Detective Luca's partner."

"But we never heard about you."

"What can I help you with?"

"You know what's going on?"

"I have the case file. May I ask why you're following up rather than Mrs. Gabelli?"

"Robin said she called but couldn't get any information."

"There's nothing to report."

"Oh. No one's looking for Phil?"

"This is an active investigation and we're pursuing a couple of leads."

Leads? What did she mean by that? "Oh, something's in the mix?"

"I'm not at liberty to discuss the case, but you can assure Mrs. Gabelli that we're continuing to determine the whereabouts of her husband."

"So, you think he's taken off somewhere."

"I didn't say that."

"Not exactly, but you said the whereabouts, and that kinda means—"

"I'm sorry, but I've got to go. You can tell Mrs. Gabelli we'll be in touch as things develop."

Develop? It sounded like they had something. The question was what.

I thanked her and said goodbye. Then I thought things over for a minute before texting Robin.

17

LUCA

I WOKE UP IN RECOVERY FEELING LIKE A SUMO WRESTLER HAD used my midsection as a trampoline. My mouth was bone dry, and there were a bunch of tubes stuck in me, scaring the hell out of me. Why so many tubes? They didn't tell me about them. Did something go wrong?

The worst was the tube up my nose; it was irritating the hell out of me. I was hazy and wanted to rip it out but could barely lift my arm up.

This was far worse than I expected. It looked to me that the doctors weren't able to make me a bladder. When they opened me they probably saw that the cancer had spread all over. Damn it, Luca, whatever luck you had just went up in smoke. I was a goner. No sense fighting the grogginess, so I just let it take me away.

A clearing throat woke me. Dr. Murray came to see me, but he seemed to be alone. I tried to see if anyone was behind him. Nobody. Dr. Lino was nowhere in sight, and my worst fears were about to be confirmed.

"How are you feeling, Mr. Luca?"

"Like I've been run over."

"You've been through a lot, but I'm certain you'll be back to normal quickly."

"If you call living with a bag of piss hanging off you normal."

Murray just stood there for a second before stammering, "I, I . . ."

"It's okay, Doc, I know you couldn't make a bladder."

"No, no, we did."

"What? Where's Dr. Lino?"

"He was called in on an emergency surgery."

"So, he, you, were able to make a new bladder for me?"

Murray smiled. "Yes, it was difficult but successful."

"I, when I didn't see Dr. Lino I figured . . ."

"Oh, I see now."

He started to laugh and I joined in, but my belly started yapping. Murray gave me a rundown on what they did. He claimed to be confident they removed all the cancer and said it had not spread to the lymph nodes, or anywhere. If I could have gotten up, I would've planted a big kiss on him. He left saying he'd be back with Lino as soon as I was moved out of recovery.

THE FOLLOWING MORNING, they had me up and walking the halls, even though I was connected to an assortment of bags and lines. It was slow going and painful. I started feeling a little better after breakfast and really turned the corner when they took the catheter out in the late afternoon.

Vargas showed up right after dinner with a card and a white orchid.

"How are you feeling, Luc?"

"Better than I expected. That's for sure."

"That's wonderful. I was worried about you, partner." She took a seat in a blue plastic chair.

"I told you it'd be all right."

"I know, but you scared me the other day. You weren't yourself."

"What are you talking about?"

"Come on, Luca, we ain't been partners for ages, but we know each other. No?"

"Yeah, guess you're right."

"So, what do the doctors say?"

"They're pretty sure they got it all." She didn't need to know about my new bladder.

"Thank God, thank God. You see, praying works."

"You'll make a believer out of me yet, Vargas."

"You're my pet project, Frank. If I can turn you around, the pearly gates will be wide open for me."

"Very funny. Hey, what happened with Tommy Thumbs?"

"This is a social visit, Frank."

"Oh, come on, I'm here only a week, and already I'm outta my mind."

"Let's just call it interesting."

"Don't play with me, Vargas. What's going on?"

"Like I said, it's a social visit, and you need your rest. We'll talk, maybe tomorrow."

Before I could protest, Vargas headed for the door. She pulled it open and turned around.

"Oh, I almost forgot to tell you." She was smiling ear to ear.

"What? Spit it out."

"Some nice young lady, well, she seemed young, called for you."

Could it have been Kayla? "Who was it?"

"Said her name was Kayla. She was worried about you. Said she was out with you when you took the nosedive."

Kayla. I had to admit I'd thought about her a couple of times, but with the medical things moving at asteroid speed and the nature of my problem it didn't seem like a good time to chat. Now I seemed to be in the clear and wanted, almost needed, to talk with her.

A nurse came in.

"How are you doing, Frank?"

"Pretty good. Do you know where my phone is?"

"Uh, no. I'll check with the desk as soon as we get done here."

"What are you going to do? Take blood again?"

She shook her head. "You've got to relieve yourself."

"I don't feel like I have to go."

"I know. That's because you no longer have the nerve system that signals it's time to go."

"Oh, yeah. I forgot about that."

The nurse helped me get up and moved the IV pole along with me to the bathroom. I turned my back to her at the bowl, and she said, "You'll have to sit, Frank."

I shook my head.

She backed out and said, "Try pushing."

I didn't feel like going, and nothing was coming out, even though I was pushing.

"I can't go. Nothing's coming out."

"It helps to raise your knees. Try getting on your tippy toes. Also rub or kinda tickle your abdomen. But be careful with the wound."

I did as she said and after about five minutes of counting the yellow tiles on the wall, a trickle of pee finally dribbled out.

"Good, Frank. Now, when you're done, try to see if you

can feel the difference in your abdomen. I know everything is sore down there, but a lot of patients learn to detect a bit of pressure when they really have to go. It'll be something to concentrate on."

"Okay, I'll try."

She wanted me to walk the halls before getting back in bed. I had no choice; my call would have to wait.

We got back in after circling the floor two times. It was tiring. The nurse dug out my phone from the room's locker, and of course it needed to be charged, and I didn't have a charger. The nurse said she'd get one for me and left.

She came back with a cord dangling from her hand and a smile beaming from her face.

"Here you go."

I took the charger and tossed it on the nightstand.

"What's the matter? I thought you wanted to make a call."

"Changed my mind." Fact was, I realized I didn't have Kayla's number. I tried to recall her last name but was so exhausted I nodded out.

18

STEWART

"Don't wait. The time will never be just right." - Napoleon Hill

WHAT DOES SHE WANT? PHIL'S NOT COMING BACK, SO MOVE on already. I couldn't understand why Robin was clinging to her old life. That was history. What, was she bullshitting when she'd say you gotta move on?

I was anxious. Could it be I was pressing things a little too fast? They were married ten years. I guess that's a long time. But Philly wasn't some devoted husband. Maybe she was just putting on a show for everybody, acting the way most people do. What you're expected to do. All the mourning bullshit as the weeks and months fly by. Fools, that's what they are. Who wants to waste years of your life holed up, playing poor me?

The head doctors all say you've got to give it time. Time heals all wounds, blah, blah, blah. Meanwhile, as the clock is ticking, your life is slipping away. That's plain stupid. If you're eventually gonna recover, why not force the rebound sooner?

Mental toughness. Take the emotion out. That's what it takes. Know what the plan is and shut the rest of the shit down.

I wish I would've realized it years ago. But looking back doesn't do anything for anybody. Robin's got to keep focused on today and maybe tomorrow. She can't be wasting anymore of her time or mine.

I had to find a way to wake her up. In need of reinforcement, I got up to grab the new inspirational quote book I bought, then I remembered Robin's birthday was coming up.

I'd have to do something nice for her. Something different. Go to a fresh place with no memories of Phil. Maybe the new place on the water in Marco. I can't remember if she'd been there. Food's a hair better than okay, but the setting is pretty sweet. A couple of cocktails with a sunset and you'd be as relaxed as liquid. I gotta ask her if she'd been there without tipping her off.

I sat down on the lanai and opened to a random page. Unreal, one of my favorite quotes:

"All men dream: but not equally. Those who dream by night in the dusty recesses of their minds wake in the day to find that it was vanity: but the dreamers of the day are dangerous men, for they may act their dream with open eyes, to make it possible."

This guy T. E. Lawrence was a genius.

WHAT THE FUCK? I couldn't believe my ears that some woman detective had come to the office asking about me. It must've been Luca's partner, that Detective Vargas. Now I gotta listen to Greely's bullshit? Maybe I should just quit, tell them to fuck off.

Nobody but Tony said anything, but I could tell the way everybody looked at me they knew the police had come. I wanted to punch that bitch Judy in the face when she said Mr. Greely wanted to see me. Her voice was dripping with contempt, like I was some street thug. She never liked me, the old bag.

Who do these cops think they are? Shouldn't they have told me they were coming? Don't they give a damn if they screw with somebody's job? I didn't give two dumps for the job, but when I go, I'm going out on my terms.

What could Greely say? He had nothing to talk about. What, I'm late every now and then. I make a couple of mistakes here and there. The cops are wasting their time, and you know what? That's a good thing as far as I'm concerned. Let them chase their tails with my job. They won't find anything there.

19

LUCA

AN AUGUST SUN SHOWER BROKE OUT AND I JOGGED, NAH floated, into the station. I felt as happy to be here as I was the first day out of the academy. I couldn't believe my eyes; everyone was standing and clapping. These people and most everyone I'd run into down here were always *off the hook* nice. But getting an ovation for being in the hospital?

I shook a few hands and thanked everyone as I made it to my little piece of real estate. It was uncomfortable for me, but I was glad to be back in my office after almost three months away.

Vargas was behind her desk, looking as good as she ever did. She had a smile as wide as the Gulf of Mexico.

"Good to have you back, Frank."

"But not good enough for a standing O like everyone else?"

She threw a ball of paper at me.

"They do this every time someone gets sick around here?"

"You didn't just get sick, bozo, you had cancer, and you've beat it."

I still hated hearing the C word. "We'll see about that."

"Don't be getting gloomy on me, Luca. My horoscope says it's going to be a surprisingly upbeat day."

I waved her off and asked, "Can you update me on the cases?"

Vargas filled me in on four drug cases, two armed robberies, and an assault, before getting to the Gabelli case. It was virtually the only case I had been thinking about while recovering.

I asked, "What did you ever find out about the bookie, Tommy Thumbs?"

She grabbed a file and opened it.

"He was tight-lipped, but no doubt that Gabelli was in deep to him."

"How deep?"

She grimaced. "Wouldn't say exactly, but said it was a lot and that he was concerned but not worried about the debt."

"Concerned but not worried? Gabelli get behind the eight ball regularly?"

Vargas nodded. "Tommy said there was a handful of times that Gabelli had an unlucky streak."

"We got time frames?"

"Said he didn't keep records, but said it was over the last two years or so. Said he was sorry to lose such a good customer."

"What was your sense of him?"

"He's creepy. I didn't like the fact he knew Gabelli was missing. When I pressed him, he said Gabelli owed him money and went looking to collect."

"Makes sense. Can't collect from a dead man."

"So why you so hot on what Tommy Thumbs had to say?"

"Gives me a better handle on what's going on. If Gabelli was into Thumbs for big wood, then chances are he was in over his head with another bookie or two. Plus, these guys play hardball to collect, and sometimes things just get out of hand and somebody ends up dead."

"It could show Gabelli was desperate if he owed to a couple—"

"Bingo, Vargas, you're learning."

"And desperate men do desperate things."

She threw one of my favorite phrases back at me. I thought it sounded pretty damn good.

"What now? How do you want to follow this?"

I said, "Why don't you go see Stewart? Ask him again about why he never said anything about his buddy Phil gambling. He may be hiding something, and I'll go see the missus and also swing by Gabelli's office."

THE GABELLI HOUSE had the new coastal contemporary look. It was off-white with dark Bahama shutters and had modern-looking garage doors with opaque windows. Everything had straight lines and a simple elegance to it. When I first started seeing the new style it felt too modern, but I came around quickly, and this one was real nice. I liked the way the pavers were laid in a herringbone pattern. I figured the home was worth a minimum of two and a half to three million as I rang the bell.

I wasn't sure what to expect, but Robin's gleaming smile and warm handshake threw me off. She was dressed in a red silky dress. Did she wear that just for my visit? The dress hugged her, outlining a body worthy of any men's magazine.

Not a straight line anywhere, I thought, as Robin showed me into a two-storied family room.

"Can I get you something to drink, Detective?"

I took a seat in a light blue armchair. "I'm okay, but thanks anyway."

She smoothed the dress where it hit her ass and sat in a swivel club chair with black piping.

"I so glad you're feeling better, Frank."

She went from detective to Frank in a nanosecond.

"Thank you. I wanted to ask you a couple of questions."

"Sure. Fire away."

"I understand that Mr. Stewart and you had an affair. What can you tell me about that?"

She crossed her arms. "There's not much to say. It was something I regret. It was over in a heartbeat."

"So, the affair didn't last long?"

"No, it did not, and I wouldn't call it an affair; it was a one-time thing."

"Did your husband know about it?"

"Are you crazy? It'd kill Phil if he knew."

"When this, shall we say, interlude ended, did things get back to normal?"

She smiled. "No harm, no foul."

There wasn't a referee in sight. "That's an unusual way of putting it."

"Look, it was stupid of me. I shouldn't have done it, but I was mad at him and things just got out of control, you know what I mean?" She crossed a leg, revealing a thigh Frank Perdue would kill for.

Having had my share of encounters, I certainly knew how things could spiral, but said, "Are you referring to the affairs that your husband had?"

"It wasn't that, or maybe some of it was that, I guess. But he was traveling like crazy. He was never home, and Dom, well Dom was there and we hung out a lot. I was lonely."

She swiveled to the left, showing a little more of the fine china before swinging back. The pout on her face and behavior was the furthest you could get from the type A she was. It crossed my mind she might be playing me.

"Was ending it a mutual thing?"

She frowned, showing the first wrinkle I'd seen on her.

"Not really."

"I assume Mr. Stewart wanted things to continue?"

She nodded. "No doubt. He kept badgering me to give it another chance."

"Badgering?"

She uncrossed her legs and leaned forward. "Look, I made it perfectly clear it was a one-time thing. I told him it was over and done with, and that was that."

I was glad type A resurfaced. As much as I tried, I didn't really trust myself to resist her if the opportunity arose.

"And Mr. Stewart backed off?"

"For the most part."

"Care to elaborate?"

"It's just that there's always something there, you know what I mean?"

Boy, did I ever. I avoided the question. I said, "You say that like you have some experience in the, uh, area?"

Did she just bat her eyes? She recrossed her legs and said, "I'm no angel, but I love my husband and don't play around."

Yeah, right. This was interesting and fun. I was glad to be back in the saddle. I explored the infidelity subject for a while, but I didn't feel any other of her transgressions had much to do with the case, so I wrapped it up and hightailed it to a McDonald's to use the restroom. No way I was going to use her bathroom.

DAMN IT. Someone was in the commode. It'd been a good four hours since I took a pee, and my abdomen was feeling the pressure and that was a no-no. The doctors told me not to mess around with pushing the time between leaks, as it could rupture the internal incisions.

After hopping around for a minute or two I banged on the door.

"Hurry up in there."

"Leave me alone, you moron."

"I gotta go bad, man."

"Tough shit."

I wanted to kick the door down and rap this guy in the mouth, but I was afraid I'd pee in my pants in the process and headed out the door. I looked both ways, scooted into the lady's room and sat on one of their thrones. It was the fastest time I got a stream going and it felt good.

The thought of sex got me down. Things weren't right down there. The doctors said it would take time, but it seemed like things were disconnected somewhere between my mind and Little Luca.

The door opened and I pulled in my feet. It had to be a young girl by the look of her sneakers. She went into the next stall and took her sweet time as I wondered if a man's breath was discernable from a woman's. After she did her business, I saw her feet by the sink. She washed, thank goodness, but didn't move. What the hell was she doing, admiring herself in the mirror?

Finally, her feet left the sink and the door swung open. I

scrambled to my feet, zipped up and cracked the stall door open. I grabbed the bathroom door and pulled it open to the surprise of an older lady on her way in.

I said, "Sorry, I thought this was the men's room."

She eyed me suspiciously, so I had to duck into the men's room for a while and fake flush before heading to the parking lot.

20

STEWART

"Expect the best. Prepare for the worst. Capitalize on what comes." - Zig Ziglar

IT WAS ROBIN. "THEY FOUND PHIL'S CAR."

Damn it. Valentine's Day was around the corner, and this would throw a monkey wrench into my plans.

"Phil's car? Where?"

"Lehigh Acres. It was stripped down somewhere off of Jaguar Boulevard."

"Oh. Did they say they have any leads about Phil?"

"No, they said it was in a place where the local gangs bring the cars they steal."

"Did they get anything off it, like fingerprints?"

"They didn't say, but this is the first piece of good news since Phil disappeared."

"It's not good news, Robin."

"What're you talking about, Dominick?"

I hated when she called me Dominick. It was so impersonal, like a room monitor at school or something.

"It could mean Phil's not coming back."

She gasped. "Oh no. Do you really think so?"

"Well, I don't want to speculate, but if he left his car behind . . ."

"It was stolen and stripped, that's what the police said."

"I hear you, but it's possible he left it somewhere, maybe an airport or someplace. If he was coming back you know he would've kept it safe or something. I don't know, maybe even sold it."

"How the hell would selling it be a sign of his intention to come back?"

"Oh, I don't know. Shit, I don't know what to think anymore. You know, I miss him like you do."

"This is a bad dream, a nightmare."

"I know, it's crazy. Hey, you wanna grab a bite to eat later?"

"What? How can you think about eating at a time like this?"

I should've waited, or called her back.

"I don't know, I just didn't want you to be alone after hearing about the car and all."

"I'm sorry, I know you're trying to help."

Man! That was a damn good recovery. Maybe Valentine's Day could be salvaged.

AROUND FIVE O'CLOCK MY cell buzzed. It was her! She probably did want to go out and eat!

"Hiya doing, Robin?"

"The cops must think Phil is dead." Her voice cracked.

I guess I'd be eating alone tonight and could forget about Valentines.

"What are you talking about?"

"Detective Luca came here with a forensics team."

"What? Why?"

"To collect Phil's DNA."

"Oh, of course. It's probably routine. I'm surprised they didn't ask earlier."

"You think so?"

"Of course. On *CSI:* they do it all the time. What did they take, a hairbrush, toothbrush?"

"Yeah, they took his toothbrush. Went through his closet and combed through the rug by his side of the bed. They even took his flip-flops."

"Makes sense. They say DNA is all over the place."

"What do you think this means?"

I had no idea, but I couldn't rule out that they might have something. "Don't panic, Rob. I really think it's routine."

"I hope you're right."

"Look, don't take this the wrong way, but I'm starving. You wanna get something to eat with me?"

"I don't feel like eating."

21

LUCA

WHEN I GOT BACK TO MY DESK, THE REPORT I'D BEEN waiting for was sitting in my in-box. I had the DNA from the car cross-checked against Florida's database of known criminals, hoping for a break in the case.

I ripped the brown envelope open. Bingo, there were two matches. As I pulled up the first rap sheet, I wondered how they caught anyone in the old days.

Twenty-six-year-old Diego Bosque had done two stints behind bars, both for grand auto theft. He'd been busted for several petty thefts, but nothing to suggest Bosque was violent. It wasn't surprising to link him to the theft of the car, but I didn't give a rat's ass about the car unless it led to what happened to Gabelli. I doubted little Diego had anything to do with the vanishing, but we'd have to check him out. Hot-hands Bosque was in Fort Myers and was going to get a visit. Hitting the print icon, I moved on.

It felt strange, but when Jamil Johnson's file came up I felt a surge of optimism. Jamil was thirty-two with a rap sheet that read longer than *The Old Man and the Sea*. Covered in jailhouse tattoos, Jamil was an ugly mother-jumper prone to violence. The thug was part of an Orlando drug gang and had been in and out of jail his entire adult life. With all the assaults, many with a deadly weapon, he appeared to be a gang enforcer.

The Orlando gang angle was confusing, though. We'd never had a run-in or even a report of gang activity from anywhere but Miami. It didn't make sense, but this Gabelli dude was complicated. Who knows what kinda crap he got himself into?

Checking the dates, I confirmed Jamil had been out on the streets when Gabelli went missing. Even though the crooked line of crime straightened a hair, this cretin was a solid four hours away. I didn't really want to be sitting in a car, hoping my bladder wouldn't burst, and come up with another zero. Besides, Vinny Colavito, an old buddy from the academy, had been on the Orlando force for the last ten years.

Even though we had never made good on the promise to get together after I moved to paradise, Colavito and I jumped right back into the dorm room days. Colavito wasn't working the gang unit, but he'd have Jamil Johnson questioned and, if there was something there, hold him.

———

GOING to Baleen for a bachelor party really threw me off. I was surprised how it affected me. It must have been obvious, as a couple guys from the station asked me if I was okay. I paused before I'd gone into the bathroom. That was where it all started.

A night filled, make that overflowing, with promise was turned upside down in less time than it took for a tissue to burn. Fact was, I didn't need the reminder of how fragile life was. I learned years ago to enjoy it when you could. But the reality was I never expected it would be my tail caught in the trap at such a young age.

It was clear to me that sooner or later everyone gets their time with misery in this life. I thought I was in touch with my death, but I was no better adjusted than anyone else walking around in denial. It was embarrassing; I'd been an outspoken advocate of planning your own funeral, even picking out your casket, as a reminder we were going to die. Turns out, like most advice, we didn't want to walk the walk. Egg on the face? I had a couple of cartons dripping off me.

Dragging me down further was the Kayla reminder. No one had to tell me it was the first inning, but there was no question we clicked. I felt we were going places together. She seemed as interested as I was. She'd reached out when it happened, so she cared. I should've tracked her down, but with my mechanics not working, it seemed futile. I don't know why I didn't reach out to her. My doctor said my physical issue could lead to depression. Maybe that was it.

I'd been going for injections to help reduce scar tissue. The doctors said that a buildup of scar tissue was responsible for dulled nerve endings that contributed to being unable to get an erection. I was hoping he was right and they hadn't cut something else down there.

He said he was one hundred percent certain that Viagra would solve my problem, but, since bladder pain and increased urination were possible side effects, he wanted to try the injections first. It made sense, but he wasn't the guy unable to get a hard-on.

My reasoning was nothing more than stupid and immature. If she was the one for me, she'd help me through this and be okay with me taking a pill to get my mojo back. Don't piss away the opportunity, Luca. Find a way to reach out to her.

I HUNG UP THE PHONE.

"Another dead end, Vargas."

"Who was that?"

"That old buddy of mine in Orlando. They brought Jamil Johnson in and hammered him. But it looks like Diego was telling the truth for a change. Jamil was seeing his cousin and he gave him a ride. Said he was going to kick Diego's ass all over Lee County for not telling him he was riding in a hot car. You can't make this shit up."

"Well, at least Gabelli wasn't mixed up in some drug thing."

"I'm gonna have Diego picked up on this."

"But we promised we wouldn't if he talked."

"We can't look the other way, this guy's too brazen. We need to take him down a couple of pegs."

"I don't know, we might need him some day."

"With his history, we'll always have plenty of bait."

22

LUCA

SIMMONS CONSTRUCTION OCCUPIED THREE FLOORS IN A GLASS office tower on 41, just south of Park Shore. For a large, international construction company, the offices were unimpressive and bordered on shabby. The chair I sat in cried to be reupholstered, and the coffee table was marred. The only redeemer was the view. I focused on a sliver of the gulf that shined in the distance until a shapely young lady asked me to come with her.

I followed her swaying tail as she escorted me to the corner office of John Conner, who was Gabelli's boss. The office was filled with models of buildings and framed architectural drawings. It was a hip-looking place to work, except it was too cold for me. Spring was a couple of weeks away, yet they had the AC blowing like mad.

Conner was a Brit, but his accent had toned down considerably in the fifteen years he'd been here. He was another one of those guys who opted to shave his head to cover balding. Conner wore thick-framed glasses and a lip beard. He looked like he collected wines. Nothing big, but he'd be a good guy to know if I was right.

"How long did Mr. Gabelli work here?"

"Phil started a couple of years after I got here, so I'd say about a dozen. I'll have HR get an exact date for you."

"What were his responsibilities?"

"He was, uh, is one of our project managers."

"What was he managing when he went missing?"

"Phil was on the Sweet Bay project."

"What type of a project is that?"

"A mixed-use development, some retail, office, and a slice of residential. It's the bulk of what we do here at Simmons."

"Where is this Sweet Bay?"

"Down in Santiago, Chile."

"I understand Mr. Gabelli did quite a bit of travelling."

"Travelling? No, Phil didn't visit the job sites. That's the superintendent's responsibilities."

"Mr. Gabelli never travelled on company business?"

"I don't like to say never, but it's been probably ten years or so since we separated things, so if he did any travelling it was a long time ago."

"That's interesting. His wife said he did a lot of travelling."

"I don't know where she got that impression. Maybe Phil could've been covering something with her."

"That's what I'm trying to figure out."

"I hope you do."

I nodded and said, "By the way, you like wine?"

His eyes gleamed. "Big time. You?"

I WAS STOPPED at the light on Vanderbilt and Airport when it hit me that I might be wasting my time. It looked like Gabelli had taken off. He had a history of disappearing for a few days at a time, usually holing up with different women. Maybe he found a new squeeze at the same time he'd run up a gambling debt and decided to run off for good. The combo seemed to be a decent motivator.

We'd been chasing this too long; it might be time to put the Gabelli case on hold. Especially now, when we could be of use elsewhere.

The department was pushing back aggressively to keep the Miami-based gangs from even thinking about crossing Alligator Alley. The effort was successful, but it drained a lot of officers from their regular duties. Nothing had gone wrong as a consequence, and the brass wanted to be sure it stayed that way. As a result, they were now asking us not to waste time on cases that were truly dead-ended. The Gabelli case seemed to qualify.

I WAITED for Vargas to get out of a meeting to kick it around with her. Unless she totally disagreed, I was going to hit the pause button on the Gabelli case. I was reading my e-mail when Sally, who manned the TIPS hotline, popped her red head in.

"Hey, Frank, call came in on the Gabelli case."

"Are you kidding me?"

She shook her head. "Some guy, who wanted to remain anonymous, said the wife is about to receive a couple-a-million-dollar payout from a policy on her husband."

"And how did he know this?"

"Said he worked at the insurer, Lincoln Life Insurance."

"Wow."

"And here's the best part; he said the policy was in effect less than two years."

"I wonder if there's a way to verify this."

"You'd probably need a court order to get Lincoln to open its books up."

"Do me a favor, Sally, and tell Vargas I'll be back in an hour or two."

———

I STRUGGLED to avert my eyes from the plunging neckline on Robin's blouse as I said hello. Boy, I liked the way they dressed in the advertising business.

She flashed a smile with her perfect teeth. They had to be bleached. Robin looked even fresher than I remembered her. Was it a bit of Botox? I tried to place her perfume as I brushed past her; it reminded me of something my wife used to wear.

We sat across each other in a conference room that was freezing. The walls were full of colorful prints by Leroy Neiman, in a poor attempt to disguise the fact the room was windowless.

"Sorry about the room, but this place is filled with nosy bodies."

"Fine by me."

"What did you want to see me about?" She tilted her head.

"Lincoln Life?"

"What?"

"It's come to my attention that you're about to collect a couple of million from a policy on your husband."

"And what about it?"

"How come you never mentioned it?"

"You never asked, and frankly it's none of your business."

"Look, when you filed that missing person report you made anything to do with your husband my business."

"What does that have to do with anything?"

"A couple of million dollars makes a pretty strong motive."

"Are you saying I did away with my husband to get the insurance money?"

Her choice of using 'did away with' rather than 'killed' was interesting. Was she subconsciously softening her actions?

"I'm not saying anything. I'm just trying to understand why, almost ten months into his disappearance, it never came up."

"It just didn't."

"Was this policy in effect a long time?"

After a split-second hesitation she said, "A couple of years."

I expected her to be nonspecific but didn't want to press her on that.

"Do you have life insurance?"

"You mean on me?"

"Yes."

"No."

"That seems a bit unusual, to have a policy on your husband but not on you, even though I understand you earn more than him."

"That's right."

"Mind explaining that?"

"I was supposed to get covered, but I never went for the medical exam and the application lapsed."

It not only made sense, but it was something I'd done

myself, despite the badgering from the insurance salesman. I moved on.

"What made you file for the payout now, while there's an active investigation going on?"

Anger flashed over her face. "Active? You got to be kidding me."

I was surprised by the outburst; it seemed genuine.

"What made you file?"

"A friend of mine mentioned it to me. She said that after a year an insurance company had to pay and that I could file ninety days before the year was up. Why shouldn't I get the proceeds as soon as I'm entitled? They had no problem taking my premiums."

"That friend happen to be Dom Stewart?"

She narrowed her eyes. "No."

"You have any plans for the money?"

"You seem preoccupied with money, Detective."

She sidestepped the bait, so I said, "In my business you learn pretty quickly that more people have been murdered over money than lust."

She smiled. "Greed is powerful."

"Hope you don't mind me asking, but exactly how much insurance was on Mr. Gabelli? Two, three million?"

"Three."

"Wow. Three million dollars. Boy, where I come from, that's a lot of money."

She shrugged.

"That was a nice commission for the sales guy."

"I guess so."

"What's the name of the salesperson?"

"Why do you want that?"

I heard a trace of panic in her voice, so I said, "Routine. Nothing specific. I don't need it."

"It's no big deal. I can try and look it up for you."

Look it up? You'd go straight to the salesperson to collect on something like this. Why try to navigate a behemoth insurance company alone?

"Okay, thanks. I guess it's the same guy you filed your application with."

"Uh, I, uh. You know what? I used a different agent than Phil."

"Really? Why was that?"

"A friend of a friend had a kid starting out and I wanted to throw him some business. You know how that is."

Friend of a friend? "That was nice of you."

"I try to help when I can."

"Only trouble is, you never went through with it, so the kid didn't make a dime."

She couldn't hide the flicker of anger that ran across her face. "Well, I tried. It's more than most people do."

I stood. "Thank you for your time, Mrs. Gabelli. When you can, I'd like the name of both insurance salesmen."

I didn't know what to make of this seesaw. It was three million dollars, and she never mentioned it? I didn't like her answers about her insurance; she was hiding something. Yet she truly seemed pissed that we'd been unable to find out what happened with her husband. She was smart, and there was no doubt she could be a bitch, but a killer?

23

LUCA

CRUISING ON GOLDEN GATE PARKWAY, I WAS HEADED TO YET another doctor visit when my radio crackled:

"Request officers in the Golden Gates vicinity to respond to a possible seventy-one underway at 16715 Tropical Way."

The address was vaguely familiar. "This is Detective Luca. Ten-fifty-one. ETA in five minutes. What can you tell me?"

"All's we know is a little kid called in saying his mother was being beaten up. It seems real, but, as usual, be on ambush alert."

By the time I holstered the handset, an uneasy feeling erupted in my belly, and it had nothing to do with my bladder. I tried to tamp down my rising fear as I turned onto Santa Barbara Blvd. The area was too damn familiar and I prayed for the best as I pulled up, knowing it wasn't a setup.

The front door was ajar and I steeled myself as I trotted up the walk, keeping my hand ready to draw my gun. Comforted by the sound of a woman sobbing, which I knew would be a redhead, I entered the house, announcing my presence as an officer. No amount of wishing it was déjà vu could change the facts. I had been here before.

A TV was on somewhere, but the family room was empty. Stepping over two overturned chairs, I headed toward the crying.

They were in the bedroom. Two little kids were whimpering in a corner near their badly beaten mother, who was sprawled on the floor. I waved to the children and knelt by the woman. Blood was oozing from a nasty cut on her cheek, and she had a bruise on her forehead.

"Ma'am, I'm a police officer here to help."

She nodded her head as I checked her pulse.

"Good. Everything's going to be okay. I'm going to call for an ambulance."

I radioed the request in and told the kids I'd be right back. Closing the door behind me, I drew my pistol and headed down the hallway. Fast asleep, in a brown corduroy recliner, was the wife beater. I scanned the room for possible recording devices but there didn't seem to be any.

Stepping quietly toward him, I barely resisted the urge to bash his cowardly face in. So, I did the next best thing. I slammed the butt of my gun into the mousy bastard's kneecap. He bolted awake, screaming in pain. Then I whacked his other knee.

I held my gun up. "Shut up or I'll put a piece of lead in you."

"I, I—"

"I told you to shut up." I turned the TV off and said to him, "You move out of this room, you're going to catch a bullet from me. You hear?"

The coward nodded. I closed the door behind and headed back to the bedroom as the EMT crew piled into the house. As they began tending to the woman, two uniformed officers arrived. The bedroom was overcrowded, so I asked the kids to step into the hall.

"You can see from over there. We just need to give these people some room to help your mother."

Then I crouched beside her. "Ma'am, we're all here to help. I just need to know that it was your husband who did this to you."

She turned her head away.

"Look, I was here a couple of months ago. Remember, when he broke your mother's vase?"

She began to cry. "He'll kill me, me and the kids, if I say anything."

"No, he won't. We're here to protect you and your children. Do you have family that can tend to the kids while you go to the hospital?"

She shook her head. "No, they're up in New Hampshire, and I ain't going to any hospital."

"You have to, you're bleeding and you've got to be checked out."

An EMT responder said, "Want me to call Family Services?"

"I don't want my kids being wards of the state! I can take care of my own kids!"

I said, "Don't worry, ma'am. I'm not gonna let your kids go anywhere. Is there a neighbor they're comfortable staying with while we make sure you're okay?"

"Mrs. Hannity loves the kids, but she works till five."

I checked my watch; it was a bit before one. Approaching the kids, I smiled as broadly as possible and said, "My name's Detective Luca. Mommy's going to go to the doctors to make sure she's all right. Since Mrs. Hannity is working, I thought we could go grab some lunch together, okay?"

The older one said, "Can't we stay with daddy?"

"I'm afraid not. You see, we're going to need his help with your mother for a while. Hey, I got a good idea, what do you say we hit the zoo after we eat?"

It was tough keeping a good face on while I was with the children. What a mess, and I'd contributed to it. No, I was responsible for today's disaster. These poor kids, chances were their father's persona non grata, and he should be. But kids, what do they know? Besides, your family is your family, and we all defend them no matter how crazy it seems at times.

Shit was piling up on me. Why did I let that beast off the hook when I could've, no, should've locked his ass up?

When the first 911 call came in was when things started sliding physically, and now, the proof was in, mentally. Was I fit enough to serve anymore?

I reached back to that day. How had I let this brute off the hook? I remembered the intermittent stabbing feeling in my gut, but I don't recall that being the reason. It's not like I hightailed it out of there because I had a lot of pain.

What did I miss? Going over it again, I really couldn't see anything. The fact was, even if I'd hauled his sorry ass in, he'd be out and about in days. And unless his wife got a restraining order, this would have happened anyway. She wasn't the type to stand up and get a court order.

Hold on, Luca, what are you doing? Letting yourself off the hook?

I felt a wee bit better thinking about the dozens and dozens of these types of cases I'd been through. The depressing fact was that it took a severe beating like this one to motivate a woman to seek legal protection. Even crazier were the countless women who defended the pond scum that abused them and resisted the advice we gave. What in the world would it take to get them to a safe place?

Man, I needed a jolt out of my funk, a chance to think and relax. Vanderbilt Beach, here I come.

24

LUCA

"MR. EAGLETON, THIS IS DETECTIVE LUCA WITH THE Collier County Sheriff. I'd like to ask you a few questions about a policy you wrote for Lincoln Life on Phil Gabelli."

"Oh, Robin said you would be calling."

"Mrs. Gabelli told you I'd call?"

"Yes, said she didn't want me to be surprised, said it was routine. It is routine, isn't it?"

"I really can't talk about it, but we're trying to learn as much as possible about Phil Gabelli."

"Of course. It's a damn shame about him, though. He was a nice guy. Healthy too."

"The policy he had, I understand the death benefit was three million. Is that correct?"

"Yes."

"How'd they arrive at that number?"

"If I recall, they originally talked about a million, but Robin wanted more. She was looking for five million, but the premiums were expensive. I suggested they do a second-to-die policy. Since they were so young, they could've gotten five or maybe even six million in coverage for the same premium."

"Second to die?"

"It's a policy where the payout occurs upon the deaths of both of the insured. When one person passes, nothing is paid, only when the second person dies. Many married couples use that type of policy."

"You suggested this to them?"

"Yes. She wanted a higher death benefit, and it was a way to get a higher dollar coverage for around the same premium cost."

"Was there a reason they didn't take your suggestion?"

"I explained the benefits of that type of policy, but Mrs. Gabelli said since they had no children it didn't make sense."

"Did it?"

"It's true that many couples use it to pass down the benefit to their heirs. But I suggested it because this wasn't a part of an estate plan."

"Did you consider it unusual that Mrs. Gabelli didn't get insured?"

"When I first talked with them, it was a typical husband-and-wife coverage situation. But when it was time for the applications, Mrs. Gabelli said she wasn't going to apply."

"She never even filed an application?"

"No, not with me anyway."

"Was Mr. Gabelli a good risk. I forget what you call it, but in good health and all?"

"Yes, he qualified for the lowest premium, which made the fact they didn't take the accidental death rider surprising."

"What's that?"

"It's quite typical, especially in younger, healthy appli-cants, that they take a rider, or additional coverage for an accidental death, say a fatal car accident. The death benefit is doubled when an accidental death befalls an insured party. In their case, the payout would jump from three to six million."

"And the Gabellis passed on it?"

"Yes. It was surprising because it wasn't expensive."

VARGAS WAS WEARING a powder-blue blouse and the herringbone slacks that I liked. But something about her looked different, better.

"You get a new hairdo, Vargas?"

"Hairdo? You're showing your age, Frank."

If she only knew that I was on the verge of asking for a prescription for little blue pills to wake up Little Luca, who had as much structure these days as an empty sock.

"Geez, just trying to pay you a compliment."

"Really? It'd be nice if you just say it then."

I felt like a jerk and changed the subject.

"After talking with the Lincoln Life guy, things just got a bit more complicated."

"What did he say?"

"First off, it was Robin who upped the insurance from a million to three. But get this, she really wanted five."

"So why did she settle for three?"

"Too much in premiums."

"That's ridiculous. If she was going to off him and collect, what would it matter how high the premiums were?"

"Good point, but maybe she didn't have the cash flow. But two other strange things came up. One is they passed on an accidental death benefit. That's a red flag in my book. It costs peanuts, and the death benefit is doubled. Why the hell would they pass on that?"

"Hmm, I don't know. You said there was another thing."

"Eagleton offered them another way to jack up the death dollars while keeping the premiums down, with something called second to die. It's where both people have to die before there's a payout."

"I don't know what that implies, Frank. I'd have to think about it, but they don't have kds, so who'd get the money when they both died?"

"Good point, but the accidental thing is troubling. Between the timing of the insurance, the amount, and the passing on the accidental death, things are starting to add up. And it points to her."

"It's somewhat circumstantial. But why don't we just ask her, see what she says?"

"She better not try to stonewall us, like she did with her husband's gambling."

25

STEWART

"The whole world steps aside for the man who knows where he is going." - Unknown

IT FELT GOOD TO FINALLY HAVE SOMETHING WORK. AFTER calling the hotline, it took less than a day for Robin to panic and look to me for comfort. Sometimes she can be so predictable. I knew they'd be looking at her, and they should. Three million bucks is three million bucks. That buys a lot of happiness from where I stand.

It was weird, though, that she passed on the accidental death thing. She said that since he worked in an office and didn't do any dangerous sports or ride a motorcycle it wasn't worth it. It seemed to make sense, but when I googled it, the top five causes had nothing to do with work or sports. It wasn't surprising that car crashes were the number-one killer, but who would've thought that choking, fires, poisoning, and falls would round out the top five. Strange, if you ask me.

The cops would have to dig deeper on the accidental thing as Robin's reasoning didn't hold together in my eyes. Not only did she stand to benefit to the tune of three million, but she was manipulative. Robin would be put under the microscope now. As far as I was concerned, she deserved to get put through the mill at this point.

Overall, I felt good about my timing. Her birthday was right around the corner, and we'd be going out to celebrate for sure. It'd be nice to have a bit more momentum going into it. Maybe it was time to tell that uppity detective something else.

Then, on top of that, I could spice things up by making her jealous. That's a surefire way to motivate a woman. It's worked in the past, and even though she's different, Robin's not that different from the others.

I remember the time I got Marilyn to fork over eight thousand to bail me out of credit card debt. We'd been going out for over a year, but asking her at least ten times for the money had gotten me nowhere. She wanted me to work things out, go to one of those debt managers and have them help get a payment plan in place.

No way I'd do that. Even if they negotiated a lower interest rate on what I owed, it would take years to pay it off. Meanwhile, I'd be living like a pauper. It pissed me off to no end that she refused to help, saying whatever savings she had were illiquid. I couldn't argue with that if it was true.

When she went to work the next day, I sneaked a look at her bank statements, which said she had over thirty-five thousand in savings, with twelve K of it in cash. When she got home I asked for a loan again. When she refused, I precipitated an argument.

After dinner, I disappeared, telling her I was meeting a friend and came home well after midnight. She was steamed. I scrawled a telephone number and name on the back of a business card, jammed it in my pants pocket, and put the jeans in the hamper.

The following evening, Marilyn began peppering me with questions about who'd I gone out with. I played into her fears by being general. It was fun pulling her around. What really got her going was the two times I set off my phone's ringtone. Each time I looked at the number and got up from the couch, whispering. When she questioned me about the calls, I said it was a just some friend from work.

Marilyn was on edge, and keeping a distance from her since we'd argued over the money was having the desired effect, but what sealed it was the receipt for a dozen roses I'd left on the counter. She confronted me, and when I confirmed a liaison, she broke down.

She wanted to know why, and I turned the money thing into a trust issue. It went as I'd scripted it, and before we went to bed, she'd written me a check.

———————

I KEPT MOVING from the lanai to the front of the house. I called and texted Robin, but the bitch didn't answer. It was such a beautiful night; it'd be a shame to waste it. The sky was streaked with purple and pink overtones as daylight ebbed away. Perfect for a ride. After changing, I jumped into my car, pulled onto 41, and headed toward Venetian Village, hoping it wouldn't be too touristy.

When I crossed Pine Ridge I made a U-turn. I was dressed real nice, and I was so close, I might as well take a drive by Robin's place—you never know. I swung onto her street. What's that, a Beemer in the driveway? Who the hell has a white Beemer?

I parked across the street and stared at her house. Whoever was there with her was in the family room, as the lights were on. When I realized the TV wasn't on, I got out and made like I was walking down the street to get a closer look. A figure passed by the big double window. It looked like a guy, but I couldn't be sure.

Then an idea hit me and I jumped back in my car and drove to the Thai-sushi joint on 41, right off Vanderbilt. I picked up a spicy tuna roll and an order of pad Thai—Robin loved the combination of noodles and crushed peanuts—and I headed back to her house.

I don't know what pissed me off more, the sexy black dress she was wearing, or the frown. It went downhill from there.

"Dom, what are you doing here?"

"I was grabbing a bite to eat at the Thai place and thought I'd bring you over a tuna roll and the noodle dish you love." I opened the top of the bag and the peanut sauce wafted up.

"We ate already."

No thank you? And who was we?

"Oh, I didn't realize you had company." I craned my neck to see inside.

A male voice called out, "Rob, everything okay?"

Rob? I wanted to shout out that things were definitely not okay, but Robin turned toward the foyer and said, "I'll be right there." Then she said to me, "Look, this is a bit uncomfortable. I've got company, and I'm sorry, but I have to ask you to leave."

"Leave? Really? A day ago, you're crying on my shoulder about the cops busting your balls over the insurance money, and now I'm persona non-grata?"

"It's not like that."

"Yeah? Then what's it like?"

"I said I've got company."

"Who's here?"

"A friend from work."

"Does this friend have a name?"

"Please, Dom, let's stop the bullshit. I don't have to answer to you."

"I try to do a good deed, and this is what I get?"

"Nobody asked you to do it."

I seethed, and it must've been the steam coming out of my ears that prompted her to say, "What you did was very sweet, Dom. I appreciate the gesture, but tonight it just doesn't work for me."

Or Mr. Office Worker.

"So, when's it gonna work for you?"

"Come on, Dom. Why don't you give me a call tomorrow? Okay?"

And just like that she closed the door. I wanted to throw the bag against the door, but instead I left it right on the front deck. Knowing it'd be overrun with bugs in twenty minutes or less gave me a tiny dose of revenge.

I sat in my car, throwing more fumes off than a twenty-year diesel, waiting for the clown to leave. By the time it hit nine thirty, the thought that this guy could be staying over put me in a panic. I leaned on the horn three times, but the only thing it brought out was a neighbor who threatened to call the cops.

As I drove home I called her cell four times, but every time it went straight to voice mail. Screw her; I dialed Melissa.

26

LUCA

I hung up the phone and shook my head. Did I miss it? Damn it. It was a fundamental, you dummy, and you never considered it? How could I have missed it? The clues were in plain sight. You knew the wife was a first-class type A. The husband disappears without a trace, and you forgot to ask about any life insurance? Mistake number one.

It took a tip from Stewart about the dough Robin was gonna collect. I didn't like the source, but information is information. Now she's in the crosshairs for a while. That's the textbook path to take.

I rolled around the investigation into the insurance procurement and benefits. There were flags, not red, but pink. How could I be so focused on her that I didn't even explore an alternative?

Was I losing my edge? Even though I felt good, despite all the bullshit I went through and was still going through, especially with my private parts, I knew deep down that the sickness changed me. How could it not? Funny thing is, I no longer saw things as black and white anymore; there was gray in life these days. Yet with the Gabelli case, I'd been looking at things as either-or.

How the hell did I miss not considering that the Gabellis planned this together? As I considered it, the possibility they conspired together blossomed. Such a conspiracy could take multiple forms:

Phil would disappear and Robin would collect the insurance. Then, after a period, Robin would disappear and join Phil wherever he was. Or Robin would collect, stay put, but split the money with Phil. Maybe Phil wanted to take off and assuaged his guilt with the money Robin would get. Or, who knows, maybe all the talk about marital problems was nothing more than a classic misdirection.

If the philandering turned out to be nonsense, I'd have to consider turning my badge in. Maybe get an inside desk job to be sure I got my pension. The union would help me. I'd use the health card. It'd be easy, as long as I could swallow my pride.

A conspiracy sure answered the questions about why there was a policy only on Phil and why they passed on the accidental death doubler, not to mention the second-to-die option. But I wasn't sold that it solved the crime. Conspiracies are tough to pull off in general, but when it revolves around a so-called missing person, it gets zillions of times harder. Where can anyone really hide today, especially with three million bucks and a lifestyle in the upper echelon? In today's world, you can't pick your nose without it being on Facebook.

Knowing all that didn't make me feel any better. It was the fact I never even considered it that shook me to my core. Rocking my boat further was the fact the new lead came from none other than Dom Stewart.

Was this guy playing with me? He was the one who

dropped the dime on the three-million-dollar insurance payout. Why didn't he tell us earlier that Phil had mentioned the life insurance scheme to him? Was Stewart some sicko watching the playout of the investigation? Did he have his eyes on Robin, and if he didn't get his way he'd sink her? If he knew about it, then he'd be a coconspirator. Hold on, hold on, Luca, you're running wild.

They'd had an affair, fling, encounter, whatever. He wanted back in, according to Robin. Only way that happens is if she leaves her husband or the husband is out of the picture. He gains nothing from an insurance scheme where Robin and Phil split the dough. Stewart can't be involved, but why the drip, drip of information? Even that gal down in the Caribbean, why did he wait to tell us about her?

Could be that's the way this guy rolls. He was tight with Gabelli and is having a tough time threading the needle. I could sympathize with him, as I'd always covered for my buddies. I'd never bury a crime, but I'd have covered the screwing around that Gabelli was doing if he were my buddy, like JJ.

I wonder what JJ would have to say about all this. Can't imagine my ex-partner and me not exploring it. We always made sure we looked under every bed.

How come Vargas never brought up the possibility? She was a good cop but not half as good as JJ. Partners look out for each other; we fill in each other's missing parts. Damn it, Vargas, why couldn't you have said something?

As if to defend her integrity, the door swung open and it was Vargas. I wasn't looking forward to telling my partner the latest.

Vargas wasn't upset at the development. Said it was progress and needed to be followed up. It may have been my reaction or the puss on my face, but she surprised me by saying it was silly and counterproductive to beat myself up over it. Of course, she was right, but I didn't like it one damn bit.

We debated whether to have Robin come down for questioning on our turf against the merits of surprising her at home. Vargas suggested we double-team her at her office, and I tried to hide that I was pissed that I hadn't thought of the idea. Was this more evidence of my slipping?

27

___

LUCA

THE RECEPTIONIST WAS PLAYING SOLITAIRE AND SNAPPED HER laptop shut when we flashed our badges. We told her we were there to see Robin Gabelli, and before she could call her, Robin walked into the lobby with the bathroom key.

She looked like she'd seen a horror movie but gave a quick shake of her head and recovered. She was good.

Her smile spread wider than the moon when she said, "What a nice surprise to see you. What can I help you with?"

Had this been the first time I'd met her I'd have bought into her Southern charm.

"We have a few things we need your help clarifying."

"I'd be happy to help. Let's go to my office."

Robin showed us into an office with a huge window that overlooked a courtyard with a fountain. Her credenza had a couple of awards and one picture of her and Phil. Her hospital-sterile desktop had a plexiglass in-box and a solitary pen on it, not a thing else.

She dialed back the hospitality. "What did you want to know?"

I said, "We'd like to go over the insurance thing."

"But I thought I answered all your questions. Believe me, I know how it looks, but despite that, it's all legitimate."

Vargas said, "We understand you received the insurance payout."

"Well, yes. They paid the benefit in accordance with the policy."

Vargas asked, "And what did you do with the money?"

"I don't think I have to answer that, as it's really none of your business, but I want to cooperate with you. The proceeds were deposited in the bank."

I weighed in, "A joint account?"

"What do you mean?"

I followed, "An account you had with your husband or just you?"

Vargas added, "Or an account with another person."

"I don't understand why you're asking. It really is none of your business."

I said, "I'll get a court order and make it my business, Mrs. Gabelli."

Robin gave me a look that had frost hanging from it. I didn't know if it was the court order or that I had addressed her formally.

She said, "Look, all along I've put up with a lot of innuendoes from the police. I didn't complain because I just wanted to know where my Phil was. But you're pushing the limits of my patience."

Vargas said, "Are you going to answer?"

"I think it's time to get my lawyer involved."

I cocked my head to Vargas and got up. Right before I opened the door I turned around and asked, "Did you and your husband plan his disappearance to collect the insurance money?"

Robin shook her head and flashed her whites. "Whatever gave you that idea?"

I said, "A friend of Mr. Gabelli's has come forward saying that your husband confided in him about a plot to have him disappear and cash in on the life insurance policy."

She blinked her eyes twice. "And who said that?"

"We're not at liberty to disclose that," Vargas replied.

VARGAS SLAMMED THE CAR DOOR. "I don't like her one bit."

Was there a tinge of jealousy in that? I pulled out of the parking space. "She's composed, you have to give her that."

"She's a phony. Playing us for fools."

I said, "Don't get me wrong, she's shifty, but I don't think they did it together."

"You think she's innocent?"

"I don't know, but I don't think the two of them planned it."

"We're talking three million dollars, Frank."

"I'm not saying she didn't do anything, just that getting away with something like that, I don't know, she just doesn't have the personality to pull something like this off."

"Oh, so now you're a psychoanalyst?"

"Just my gut, Vargas, just my gut. I don't want to brag, but most times it's a heck of lot better than some head quack, and much better than using a horoscope."

"Very funny."

"Let's keep our eyes on the money. If any or all of it moves, that'll tell us."

"Maybe, but the problem is she can take off and move the money after she's gone. They can move money around like lightning these days."

"But if she sends half to Phil Gabelli and stays around we'll never know. We should get a court order to watch her account."

"I wish it were so easy. No court's gonna give it without more evidence of a conspiracy."

28

STEWART

"No matter what happens, it is within my power to turn it to my advantage." - Epictetus

WATERSIDE WAS MY FAVORITE PLACE TO SHOP. THEY HAD every high-end store in the world. I couldn't wait to be able to shop at Ferragamo. They're the top of line, even better than all the other luxury shops in Waterside.

I headed past the water feature after leaving Saks. It was not my favorite, but my Nordstrom's card was maxed out and I wasn't getting embarrassed again. Time to drop my bags in the car and grab something to eat.

Pausing at the curb, I looked left to make sure no car was coming. What? Sitting at a high-top table on the sidewalk at Brio was Robin and that frigging guy from work. She had a drink in her hand and was leaning over the table talking.

Mr. Office Guy had blue chino pants and a Tommy Bahama shirt on. Give me a break, man, the Tommy Bahama craze ended a decade ago. I couldn't believe she was with someone like him. This guy had his legs crossed like some Ivy Leaguer. Who crosses their legs at a high-top table? No doubt this guy was a stiff. What the hell was she doing with him?

Could it be just a business thing? If so, why was Robin smiling like a cheerleader? I got to my car, threw my newly purchased clothes in the trunk, and pulled out of the space. I circled the lot for another spot. Why is this lot always so frigging packed?

A car was backing out of a spot with a decent sight line of Brio. I pulled in. A black-aproned waiter was setting down plates. I couldn't tell if Robin got the Mahi salad she usually ordered. Damn, there was a bottle of wine on the table. Was that there before?

They were doing more talking than eating. I took a swig of water to wash down the bile running up the back of my throat. As I capped the bottle, a busboy cleared their table. Mr. Office Man signaled for the check, raising my spirits.

The check came, Mr. Office Man put some cash down and they got up. As they walked out, I did a double take. They were holding hands. What the hell was going on? They stopped at the valet area. This guy valets his car at a mall? I jumped out of the car and made a beeline for the valet station.

Robin's smile collapsed into a frown as I approached. She took a baby step away from her date. Ah-ha, she knew she was doing something wrong. I almost got hit by a valet driver in a Bentley.

She said, "Oh, hi, Dom."

"What are you doing?"

"What do you mean? We just had dinner."

Mr. Office Man said to Robin, "Is everything all right?"

"Mind your own business," I said to him, and then to her, "I called you ten times. You never got back to me."

"I'm sorry, but it's been crazy at work."

I looked at her date and said, "You're telling me."

Her date said, "Look, I don't know what you want, but I'd ask you to please leave us alone."

"Shut up and stay out of this or you'll regret it."

"Dom! Come on now. I'll call you tomorrow, okay?"

"Listen to the lady, my friend."

I turned to her date and shoved a finger in his chest. "I told you to shut up and stay the hell out of my business. You keep it up and I'll wipe the floor with your scrawny ass."

The valet kid rushed over. "Sir, can I help you with anything?"

"Yeah, run this guy over, will you?"

All eyes were on me as I walked over to California Pizza Kitchen. I sat at the bar and ordered a brew and watched Robin get into a Mercedes S-Class. When they pulled away I left, without taking a sip of beer.

SHOULD I SEND HER FLOWERS? Why should I? I didn't really do anything wrong; she was the one out on a date. Maybe I embarrassed her at the valet? It wouldn't have gotten as heated if Mr. Office Man would've minded his own business. Why did people have to stick their noses into someone else's business?

He's lucky I didn't flatten his ass. Me too, I guess, otherwise I'd be crawling out of a deeper hole with her.

Her 'I'm busy at work' line was pure bull. She had three million glorious dollars in the bank, on top of what she had already. That was pretty close to 'I can tell you to go to hell' money.

Robin was making things difficult and confusing. Unfortunately, it wasn't because she was playing hard to get. Maybe it was the grieving thing.

I had to think this through. Was giving it a couple of days a good idea? I hated being out of the picture. Should I call her or go to her house?

Should I play it cool? I couldn't do the groveling thing, besides, what would I do? Nothing. She's the one who was running around. Robin better not be sleeping with him. I should've gone to her house. Why the hell didn't I do that? You're in the dark now, Stewart. You screwed up, dummy! Okay, think it through, dig deep.

You gotta take action. Can't just let this ebb away. You want something, you gotta go for it. All in or none in. No more bullshit. Got to deal with this head-on. Smooth things out without compromising too much. Yeah, that's the solution. Besides, her birthday is in a couple of weeks, and that plan is rock solid.

I picked up the phone to place an order for two-dozen roses. She'll be home in an hour. If I timed it right we could be eating dinner by seven.

29

STEWART

"Go confidently in the direction of your dreams. Live the life you have imagined." - Henry David Thoreau

SHE'S GOING TO GO CRAZY WHEN SHE OPENS THIS. EVEN THE pink wrapping paper is her style. Should I put a bow on it? Maybe even some ribbon around it? I don't know, it's a pretty small box; it'll look messy and crowded. Maybe I should put it in a larger box. That would really throw her off. Otherwise, she'd definitely know it was jewelry.

I could put it in a box and then in another box. That'd blow her mind. I'll drag it out and show her how much effort I put into it. There was that box all that stuff from Amazon came in. It's kinda big, though, and too bulky to open at a restaurant table.

What about using a shoe box? Yeah, that would work, and it wouldn't be bad to take into the restaurant. I can see it now, her opening the first box up, but maybe she won't like the theatrics. Robin's kinda serious, especially these days. You know what, forget it.

The ring will fit in my pocket. Things don't go the way I

want, maybe I don't give it to her then. I think she'll like it, though, and a ring is real personal. It wasn't like an engagement ring, but it was a damn good stepping stone.

———

Robin said she didn't want to go to Marco Island, so I booked a special table at 1500 South by the marina. It was a cool-looking place, all white leather, and it definitely smelled high end. As I approached the restaurant, I was still miffed that she had insisted on meeting me there, making the money I spent on detailing my car a total waste.

I parked under the hotel and walked over to 1500 South. Where the hell was she? The booth I reserved was empty. I checked with the hostess, and she brought me to a table by the piano, where Robin was tapping away on her phone.

"Hello, birthday girl."

She smiled a decent-sized smile. "Oh hi."

"Let's move tables."

"Why? This is fine."

"No way. I reserved a special table, a booth overlooking the marina."

"This is okay, Dom, don't make a big deal about it."

"No, it's not. It's your birthday, and after all you've been through, it's just not good enough."

This was good. The screw up with the table turned into an opportunity to show her I had standards, especially when it came to her. The night was off to a great start.

We decamped to a curved, white leather booth with black piping. The booth was positioned facing the water. It was the primo spot in the restaurant, as long as there were no loudmouths at the bar.

I checked the wine menu and ordered a bottle of the mid-priced champagne.

"Pretty nice here, isn't it?"

She nodded. "I always liked it down here, but I wonder why no restaurant ever seems to make it here."

"It's off the tourist map."

We chatted about the prior restaurants that inhabited the space until the bubbly arrived. We clinked glasses and I went to give her a kiss, but she only offered me her cheek. Uh-oh. I wondered if I should give her the ring to warm her up.

A big-assed yacht was maneuvering its way into the marina and I pointed. "Check that one out. Man, that's a beauty."

"Wow. It's huge."

"Yeah, big but slick looking."

"It must be expensive."

"You can get one of those."

"What are you talking about?"

"With the insurance money. You can afford that, or anything else you want."

"Boats are nice, but everyone says they're a headache."

"You know the saying: 'The best days to own a boat are the day you bought it and the day you sell it.'"

"Boats require a lot of maintenance. I say it's better to have a friend with a boat."

"If you're thinking about getting one, don't worry, I'll take care of it for you. I'll be your skipper."

She smiled. "Thanks, but no thanks."

To getting a boat or me being her skipper?

Robin wasn't her old self, but she seemed to have moved past the incident at Waterside. It was going pretty good, I thought, as I studied her. Her cheeks got rosier as the bottle disappeared, and the vibe got looser as it always does with booze. We both had the expensive snapper, and it was great. She didn't want any dessert, so I ordered a glass of Malbec to extend the night out and went to the john.

I liked the sparkler they put in the lime pie, though it was leaving a bunch of dark specs on the skimpy piece of pie. We sang "Happy Birthday" to her, and the sparkler died out during the chorus. I really liked the sparkler; it reeked class.

As soon as the waiter left I dug out the ring and put it on her plate.

"Happy birthday, sunshine."

She seemed surprised but didn't touch the box.

"Go ahead and open it."

She opened it as if she were defusing a bomb. I thought the red ruby showed great against the black velvet it sat on.

"It's nice. You didn't have to get me anything."

"I know, but I wanted to."

"I appreciate it, though it really wasn't necessary."

"You like it?"

"It's stunning."

"Well, put it on then!"

She put the ring on her pinky finger. What was that?

I said, "You mean a lot to me, you know."

"I know, Dom."

"We should spend more time together, like we used to."

"I don't know if I'm ready, Dom."

"Ready? What's that supposed to mean? You got to seize things when you can."

"I know, but it feels like Phil went missing only yesterday."

"It's been a year, and it didn't stop you from going out with that patsy from the office."

She glared at me. "What I do is none of your business."

"Well, two can play that game."

"What game?"

I was glad I saw the danger sign flashing ahead for a change. "Just forget it. I'm sorry I brought it up. I really understand how difficult this has been for you, Robin, and I just want to help."

Atta boy! She softened immediately.

ON A SCALE OF TEN, the birthday dinner was a fat five. Zero movement. Time's a wasting, and time I ain't got. Got to explore my options. That Melissa had three out of four of what I was looking for. She was no Robin, but her old man, who owned three Ford dealerships, was 'off the hook' loaded. Her body was an eight, eight and a half maybe, but her face was six and a half at best.

Melissa liked me for sure. I resisted her continual overtures, excepting a couple of recent ones. Come on, a guy's a guy. Maybe it was time to ramp it up. After all, what's the downside? I get to jump on Melissa's bones while making Robin jealous. Time for her to eat the food she made. If it didn't change things with Robin I'd move on. Melissa was a good, no, outstanding alternative. Either way, I'd be riding high soon.

I grabbed a beer, sat on the lanai and pulled out my cell. It was late, so I'd text Melissa and let her know I was coming in tomorrow to take her to lunch, and who knows, maybe go shopping for a new Mustang.

30

LUCA

To say the doctor's office was jammed was putting it mildly. I signed in and grabbed two magazines before settling into the last seat, which was under the TV. I started to doze off when my cell rang. It was Vargas.

"Where are you?"

"Sitting in my doctor's office."

"Oh, are you feeling okay?"

"Fine, I had a scan, but it's just routine. What's up?"

"You sure?"

"Of course, I'm sure, Mommy. What's up?"

"I'm down at Clam Pass. They found a body in Outer Clam Bay."

"A boating accident?"

"Afraid not, the body was weighed down."

I stood up. "I'm on my way."

"Don't you dare, Frank! You stay there."

"Why not? You forget that I'm the leading homicide—"

"Hold on. You need to take care of yourself. This guy's dead already. Come on down after you're done."

"But this place is packed. It'll take another—"

"Listen to yourself. You're a good detective, Frank, but nothing's gonna change with or without you around."

"You're a real sweetheart, ain't you?"

"I'll see you later, after you're done with the doctor."

"Make sure the scene is secure."

"This isn't my first rodeo, Frank."

"I know, I know."

"I'll see you later."

I pleaded, "Call me if anything comes up. Okay, Vargas? Hey, Vargas, you there?"

I FINALLY GOT to Clam Pass as the crime scene investigators were taking off their protective clothing. I'd missed a critical part of the investigation and was pissed. Seeing the scene before it was trampled on was a huge advantage. The best opportunity to try and recreate what could have happened was lost. Now I'd have to wait until the place cleared out to envision away.

The pee-pee alarm on my cell phone sounded as I got out of my car. I hit the snooze button and ducked under the yellow crime-scene tape. It was breezy and the palm trees were dancing a bossa nova.

Wearing a blue pantsuit, Vargas was talking with Darren Grumman, who led the forensic team. Grumman was a mousy guy who never gave you anything until it was fully processed. He never appreciated that we had to move quickly. As a result, half the time we figured things out without him.

Grumman was outfitted in his usual cheap, beige seersucker suit.

"What did I miss?"

Vargas said, "A kayaker spotted the body about ten thirty and called it in." She raised her arm and pointed. "It was wrapped in plastic and weighed down under the mangroves about ten yards from the boardwalk. Forensics cut the plastic away and the body's pretty much intact but covered in a waxy type thing no one's seen before. It looks to be an important clue."

Nodding, I asked, "Male?"

"Yeah, male, Caucasian, about six foot, one hundred seventy to two hundred."

I looked at Grumman. "Any idea on age?"

"Difficult to say."

"I know it's difficult, that's why you guys are here."

Mr. Helpful shook his head and walked away. Vargas said, "You know, sometimes you can get more with candy than vinegar, Frank."

"Hey, I'm at a disadvantage, not only am I late, thanks to you, but I don't have your good looks."

"What did the doctor have to say?"

No way I'd tell her he was ready to stick a needle in Little Luca to try and wake him up. "Good as new. Any idea on how old? Sounds like someone in decent shape."

"Tough to say, but Simmonelli said he thought the victim was around forty."

I flipped through the rolodex in my head as Vargas said, "They're pretty much done."

"I can see that."

She frowned. "Look, I gotta run. I'm due in court in under an hour."

Vargas handed me a drawing of the crime scene and I said, "Hustle along then. I need to do my thing."

I took a couple of deep breaths and slowly surveyed the scene until my alarm went off again. A handful of people were still hanging around, so I walked over to the hotel, which bordered the parking lot, to use their pool bathroom.

By the time I emptied my bladder there was only one officer left, and his role was to guard the crime scene.

The parking lot for Clam Pass was at the end of Pine Ridge. At the end of the lot there was a long boardwalk that passed over the bay and led to a nice strip of beach. The boardwalk was so long that golf cart shuttles, run by the adjoining hotel, transported most of the beachgoers.

I walked the area, all pavement, so no tire tracks or footprints to look for if this was a new crime. I wondered how long it took the uniforms to get the sun worshippers off the beach to clear the parking lot. Not the best PR for a town known as paradise.

After picking out the sole CCTV camera, I checked its sight line. I looked up at the hotel, but as expected, at their room rates, none of the rooms had a view of the lot. Circling the perimeter of the lot I couldn't find any other access points.

Drawing in hand, I headed to the boardwalk. The body had been weighed down in a secluded area only about twenty yards from the gazebo where the tram stopped. There were three plausible ways the poor sob ended up in the muck. He could've been walking on the boardwalk when he was attacked, maybe a robbery gone wrong, and then dumped.

Problem was he was weighed down and tied up. That suggested that if it was a robbery then the thief was ready to kill and dump the body, requiring a highly unusual robber. I didn't buy it. So, the odds at this point were that whoever did this was planning to kill this guy the entire time. It had to be. I didn't feel it was a morphing kind of situation.

He could have been lured there to be murdered, but unless there was a record of a car being left that remained unclaimed, my suspicion was that the body was transported here. Now the question was how. By car or a boat of some kind?

I started leaning toward a car being used. It just gave the killer more flexibility, that is, unless the killer had access to a remote place to launch a small boat and navigate to where he dumped the body. Nah, if he was in a remote place to begin with, why not hide the body there? Why risk it?

I tucked the boat theory in a pocket to explore later. Killing wasn't rational, so you had to be on guard for other irrational behavior.

The autopsy should help narrow things down, giving us a reasonable time frame to work with. The wax thing was something the lab guys would figure out quickly, providing us with a lead. Hoping we'd get more than that from the autopsy and forensics, I pulled out my cell. We'd need to go through the camera footage of the parking lot and see if the hotel or anyone else had any cameras. But first I'd call the Collier County Parks department to be sure any CCTV footage was held intact and was made inaccessible to anyone but the police.

31

LUCA

WE PULLED UP TO THE HOUSE AND SAT QUIETLY FOR A MINUTE before I said, "You ready?"

Vargas said, "As ready as I'll ever be with these things."

We walked up the driveway as the sun reappeared after a brief shower. The house looked even better then I remembered, making me wonder if she had done some new landscaping or something. I tried to recall the last time I was here and hit the bell.

Robin opened the door wearing a multi-colored dress. I normally didn't like what I called 'Florida' dresses, but this gal would look great in a Whole Foods bag.

Her smile evaporated when she saw us. "Oh, hi. Is something going on?"

Vargas said, "May we come in?"

She hesitated. "Of course. But please, tell me what's going on."

Vargas commented on the furnishings as we took seats in the great room.

"I'm sure you're not here for the decor, so why don't you tell me what's going on?"

I quelled the willies in my belly and said, "I'm sorry to inform you that the body found in Clam Pass was your husband, Phillip Gabelli."

Robin fell back and covered her mouth. "Oh no!"

Vargas got up and kneeled in front of her. "We're sorry for your loss, Mrs. Gabelli."

Robin's eyes moistened. "I could feel it from the minute he disappeared."

Vargas was ready with a pack of tissues and said, "Is there someone you can call to come over and stay with you?"

Robin shook her head. "I don't need anybody. Frankly, I'd been expecting this. What happened to him?"

I said, "We don't know for sure."

"Did he drown?"

"No."

Robin dabbed her eyes with a tissue. "You think he was murdered?"

"We believe so."

"Why? Was he shot? Or stabbed?"

I swallowed before saying, "He was weighed down beneath the water."

Robin sniffled. "Oh, my poor Phil. What did they do to you?"

"We're going to have to do an autopsy. It's standard in all suspicious deaths."

She nodded. "Okay, I understand."

Before I could say anything, she said, "Why would anyone want to hurt my Phil? He was a sweetheart."

Vargas said, "We're going to see to it, that whoever did this, is brought to justice."

I said, "I know this is a lot to handle, but we'll need you to identify the body, Mrs. Gabelli. I realize this comes as a shock, but the sooner the better because we'd like to do the autopsy as soon as possible."

"Where is he?"

"At the medical examiner's, on Domestic Avenue off of Industrial."

Vargas said, "I would be happy to take a ride with you. You shouldn't have to drive alone."

"You want me to go now?"

"Only if you feel comfortable with it. We're not trying to rush you, we just want to conduct the autopsy as soon as possible so that we can release his body to you."

Robin buried her face in her hands and cried. Vargas rubbed her back for a minute until she regained her composure.

Robin blew her nose and said, "I'll go see Phil now. I just need, say a half hour, to get ready."

"Would you like me to ride with you?"

"Thanks, but that won't be necessary. I'll be fine."

"Okay then, we'll meet you down there."

VARGAS and I waited for Robin in the beige, low-slung building that housed the medical examiner's facility. We continued to discuss Robin's reaction to the news in the lobby, keeping an eye on the door. We both felt that Robin reacted normally when we advised her about finding Phil's body. Sometimes a suspect is just a little too scripted when the inevitable news is delivered.

Wearing a black pantsuit and low heels, Robin paused before entering the building. Vargas went to the door and escorted her to the family room. I went to the receiving room to make sure the body was ready for viewing.

Gabelli's body was rolled out of the stainless-steel refrigeration room into the center of the smallish viewing room. I picked up the phone to let Vargas know it was showtime. As the door opened I drew a deep breath. Vargas trailed Robin by a hair as she approached the sheet-covered gurney. I looked Robin in the eye and, lip quivering, she nodded.

I drew the sheet down to her husband's neckline and Robin gasped as a wave of nausea rolled over me. Robin broke down and I quickly covered Phil's face, knowing there wasn't an undertaker in the world that could make his funeral an open casket one.

32

STEWART

"What matters is not the idea a man holds, but the depth at which he holds it." - Ezra Pound

"OH NO, DOM, PHIL'S DEAD."

"What?"

"Detective Luca came over. He said the body found in Clam Pass was Phil."

"Oh no, I'm so sorry, Robin. What did they say happened?"

"He was murdered."

"Murdered?"

"I can't believe anyone would want to hurt Phil."

I thought, really, Robin? Phil was a pretty good guy, but you knew he was cocky assed and only looked out for himself. She knew he pissed people off and was 'over the top' selfish to boot.

"There's a lot of crazy people out there."

"They want me to go identify the body."

The body? I choked down my fear and forced myself to ask, "Do want me to come along with you?"

"No. That's okay."

"But Robin, it's a very, uh, difficult thing to have to do alone. Let me come with you."

"Thanks, but it's okay."

Robin sounded good—strong. She was as smart as they come. Even though we never talked about it, she seemed to know Phil wasn't coming back.

"Okay, but if you change your mind, I'm there for you."

"You know they're going to do an autopsy."

"Really? Why?"

"Detective Luca said it was standard in murder cases."

"Oh, I feel terrible for you and Phil."

"It's going to be all right, I just wanted to let you know what was going on."

Atta girl!

"Give me a call if you change your mind. I'll be there in a flash for you."

I DROVE past Hodges Funeral Home two times before pulling into the parking lot. My original plan was to get there early so I could be a concrete pillar for Robin, but I was never good with funerals, and this one had really turned me into jelly. Florida funerals, with everyone in black, felt as off as going to the beach on Christmas Day. I had my Zegna suit on, even though it needed to be pressed, with a crisp white shirt and blue tie. It felt appropriate.

A group of guys we hung out with had arrived the same time I did and I attached myself to them like a pilot fish to a shark. We entered and were greeted by the smell of stale air infused with floral overtones.

All of us dutifully signed the register book, another stupid tradition. I mean, who goes over it? Do what with it after the funeral? Check if Johnny so-and-so came? So what if he did or didn't. What are you going to do, not go to his wake if he didn't come to one of yours?

I took comfort in the loud chatter in the room. Robin was smiling as she chatted with a group of her coworkers. Dressed in a long black dress, she looked good, even without any makeup. Sitting on top of a brown casket was a large heart-shaped arrangement proclaiming *My Beloved Phil.* Man, was I glad it was a closed casket.

As I approached her to pay my respects, I started crying. I made sure Robin saw the tears before I hugged her. I think she was wearing the new Dior fragrance. She pulled away too quickly, in my opinion, and I went and knelt before the casket. I had my eyes closed the entire time and counted to forty before getting up and heading out to the lobby.

I stood in the lobby for two hours and only came back in the room when a minister held a brief service. Phil was going to be cremated, and I was thankful to be spared having to attend a burial.

33

LUCA

I turned off Industrial Way onto Domestic and made a right into the parking lot of a typical Floridian building built in the nineties. Tossing my police pass onto the dashboard, I headed in to see the county medical examiner.

A Virginian, Dr. Bosco had come down to Naples fifteen years ago, about a dozen years before I joined the Collier County Sheriff's department. The Collier position was an easier gig than working in D.C., where there was no shortage of suspicious deaths, and it allowed Bosco to get plenty of tee time.

The building housed three autopsy suites. The main suite had space for three autopsies, while the single suite was more private, if having your body dissected and studied could ever be considered private. The third suite was for possibly contaminated victims and those who died in fires.

Bosco led me to the solo area.

"Thanks for coming down, Frank. I thought this was going to be routine, but a couple things stood out."

I squinted as Bosco turned up the lights. The coroner grabbed a clipboard off the stainless-steel dissection table and pulled down the sheet covering the body. Pretty boy Gabelli was nowhere to be found.

Bloated with some decay, the face was almost beyond recognition. It was a wonder Robin had ID'd it.

Blowing out a deep breath, I said, "Geez, Doc, I've seen my share, but I never even heard of, much less ever saw a body with adi—. How do you say it?"

"Adipocere. It's only the second time for me, so don't feel bad. First time I saw this was on a body they pulled out of the swampy area by the Meadowlands. After that I looked into it. There's even a body they call the Soap Lady, at the Mutter Museum in Philly."

"Unbelievable."

"Sure is, and it can preserve a body for centuries."

"Incredible."

"Normally, there wouldn't be much left of a body in the gulf after a week or two, so we're kinda lucky here. The way the body was wrapped and the silt covering it created the condition for this hard, waxy substance to form." Bosco tapped the grayish waxy substance covering Gabelli's forehead with a probe. "As you can see, there's some decomposition and damage from scavengers, but it's been severely limited by the adipocere."

"It's bizarre. Where does it come from?"

"Essentially, it's a conversion of the body's fat."

"What a way to end up."

Bosco nodded.

"Doc, you said some things stood out."

"First off, the victim was dead when he was put in the water."

"I figured that, but how can you be certain?"

"There was no water in his lungs, confirming he wasn't breathing when he was dumped in the water."

"How much time do you think it was between death and being put in the water?"

Bosco frowned. "Virtually impossible to say, Frank. Adipocere formations limit our ability to estimate the post-mortem interval with any accuracy. Temperature plays a large role, and since we don't know when the body was put in the water, I had to use an annual average of Outer Clam Bay and came up with a range of six to nine months."

"That's a lot of hedging, Doc."

"The body is displaying an advanced case of adipocere. That's the best I can do."

"Fair enough, Doc. What about wounds, are there any wounds?"

"No. The cause of death at this point is a massive cardiac failure."

"A heart attack?"

"Yes, but something's bothering me." He checked his clipboard. "This fellow seemed to be in excellent health. No signs of heart disease, arterial condition normal for a forty-year-old male."

"And?"

"It does happen, but it's very rare that a healthy heart just blows out on its own."

"Could it be drugs, like cocaine?"

"It could be. I tried to check, but see here."

Bosco took a scalpel and used its handle to probe Gabelli's nasal cavity.

"It's impossible to tell if the inflammation was caused by the salt in the water or existed as a precondition."

"Gabelli was a partier, but as far as we know, there was no history of excessive drug use."

"I've seen my share of so-called casual users get carried

away and end up here or, if they're lucky, the emergency room."

"I hear you, Doc. Can you tell me how long till you know what happened?"

"We'll have to wait to see how the blood panels come back."

"Okay, Doc. But keep a lid on the cause of death."

34

LUCA

I ROLLED MY HEAD AROUND AND MASSAGED THE BACK OF MY neck before beginning. Spending hours looking at grainy CCTV footage would make for bad television, but it'd be nice if the networks would occasionally show the tedious, mundane side of things.

Science had the spotlight, but most crimes were solved with a solid ground game: combing a crime scene for minutia, interviewing hundreds of uninteresting people, and, like today, hunching over herky-jerky surveillance video.

Knowing the bad guys usually cased a place in advance of their nasty deeds, I'd started two weeks before Gabelli vanished. It was hard to conceal a body, and even harder to keep a kidnapping quiet, so even though chances are he was murdered close to the disappearance date, I'd requested the footage for a month after he was reported missing.

Six weeks, forty-two long days, over a thousand hours of tape to review. I'd need a chiropractor and glasses before I finished. Farming out some of it, even to Vargas, was not in the cards. My unshakable belief was you'd miss the subtleties of something out of place if you didn't view the entire lot yourself.

The footage between 10 a.m. and 4 p.m. could be viewed in fast-forward mode, saving me some time. The camera was positioned halfway in the parking lot, angled to the right, pointed toward the entrance to the boardwalk. The bad news was that a blind spot in the left-hand corner, closest to the wooded area, would slow me down. I'd have to be careful with people parking in that area, making sure they were beachgoers and not up to anything sinister.

I inserted the first DVD and hit play. Grainy, black-and-white images of cars entering the Clam Pass parking lot two weeks before Gabelli went missing came stuttering to life. I didn't expect much, but kept my eyes out for anything unusual. You'd think anyone contemplating such a serious crime would think to blend in, but people make all kinds of stupid mistakes.

FOUR DAYS and countless DVDs had gone by without producing the slightest suspicion in the period before Gabelli disappeared. The only thing I learned was the rhythm of Clam Pass beachgoers. It had a small parking lot, so there wasn't a lot of in and out going on. The early crowd liked to get to the beach no later than ten, then it quieted down till around two, when about thirty percent of the early birds started leaving. Then around three thirty a late crowd would stream in, most of them staying till sunset.

I was glad I'd come to the day Gabelli could've been dumped in the brackish water. As I poured a cup of coffee, I remembered there was no way I'd be able to speed up the footage as much and headed to my office.

Mug of java in hand, I dropped the first 'after' DVD in. Nothing but sun worshippers. By the middle of the second DVD the sun began setting. As the light changed, I leaned forward. The parking lot emptied. I sped the tape up, and as the time stamp passed 11 p.m. a light-colored Honda Accord pulled into the lot. Slowing it down, I saw it was a male driving. I zoomed in but couldn't make out if there was anyone else in the car.

I cringed as the Accord pulled into the blind zone. Was this just a lovers' rendezvous? I studied the screen as time passed. Just after 12:40 a.m. the Honda came back into view. This time I saw a female in the passenger seat just as my pee alarm went off. I ignored it even though my eyes were stinging and hit fast-forward.

A few minutes after 5 a.m. an old van, that looked to be a Pontiac, pulled into the lot. The van seemed cautious, moving slowly until it parked near the entrance to the boardwalk. No movement. Was this just nothing more than some horny kids?

The driver's door swung open and I held my breath as a medium build, Caucasian male got out. The driver looked around and walked to the other side of the van and disappeared from sight. I hit the fast button, but as soon as I did he emerged, backing up as he maneuvered something.

Was this the guy? I hit pause and zoomed in on the license plate. I jotted down the number of the Florida tag, JF3974X, and hit play. What was that? The guy was steering a boat-like object on a wheeled caddy or wagon. He pulled on the handle and vanished down the boardwalk. I stopped the tape.

Was there a body hidden in the contraption? Did it look like the guy was dragging the 170 pounds that Gabelli was? If not, what the hell could this guy be doing at that time of the night? The warning to relieve myself sounded again but I snoozed it. I had to see what happened with this guy and sped the tape up.

The time stamp crossed 7 a.m. and the first of the day's visitors arrived. They were one of several beach walkers who trickled into the lot. This guy was gone for two hours already. Would it take that long to dump a body? That's a lot of time. Maybe he ran into somebody and had to delay dropping Gabelli near the mangroves. As I tossed the idea around, he came into view towing his boat.

Did it seem lighter? Did it look different? I moved inches away from the screen as he disappeared at the van's side. Recall Luca, recall.

As a pair of bikers cycled to the bike rack, he emerged and got back in the driver's seat. Before the van pulled out of the lot I picked up the phone, called the plate in, and headed to take a leak.

35

LUCA

I stared at the DMV photo of Richard Blake. The thirty-five-year-old didn't have a record. Curly headed, the license put him at six foot and a hundred and sixty pounds. A Pontiac Montana van was registered in his name at 1099 Barcamil Way. Checking the address, it turned out to be in Colliers Reserve, an older neighborhood known as a full-time haven, which was weird, as I never knew anyone who lived there. I had heard there weren't any condos there, and the fact Blake was collecting unemployment didn't add up. It would have been nice to go see him with Vargas, but she was due in court, and this couldn't wait.

Colliers Reserve had a different feel. The streets were lined with mature trees, but they weren't tropical types. It felt like I was driving in Georgia or someplace like that. The home at 1099 Barcamil Way was another two-tone, white and beige home about twenty years old. Its vegetation was over-grown, like all the others on the block. I wondered if the owners realized it was jungly or if it'd happened so slowly they got used to the crowded look. The house was worth a million or 1.1 at most, in my opinion. Anybody buying this home would have to dump a boatload of updates into it.

Blake's face had the healthy, weathered look of a surfer. He looked like an athlete and was surprised to see me. Blake quickly ran a hand through his sandy hair to neaten it when I introduced myself.

"What's this about, the robbery at the casino?"

Casino? The Seminole Casino Gabelli used to frequent? "Maybe. What do you know about it?"

"Not much. I was dealing blackjack in the back by the baccarat section when it happened."

"You work at the Seminole Casino in Immokalee, right?"

He nodded. "For about seven years now. I thought that was why you're here."

"I'm here about Phil Gabelli." Blake blinked but other than that there wasn't a tell. "You know him?"

"Gabelli? Can't say it rings a bell."

What was this guy, a lawyer? "You were observed in the early morning of May first at Clam Pass. Can you tell me what you were doing there?"

He pulled his chin in. "Observed? You had someone watching me back in May?"

"Security cameras at Clam Pass filmed you. What were you doing there?"

"Who remembers that far back? But it's a public park. I have every right to be there."

"Look, we can do this the easy way, or I can drag you to the station and we can talk there. Either way you want to do it is fine by me."

"I didn't do anything wrong. I'm sure I just went out for a sail."

It was a boat. "Sailing before dawn?"

"I work the night shift, and a lot of times I can't sleep."

"So, you drag your little Sunfish out and go sailing in the dark?"

"If you knew how beautiful it was when you're on the water when the sun comes up, you wouldn't be so smug."

"How long do you go out for?"

"Depends, but usually two, three hours."

"You take a lot of things out with you?"

Blake stared at me. Did I hit a nerve?

"What are you talking about?"

"What do you take out on the water with you?"

"Not much, something to eat."

"You just sit there in the dark?"

"It's peaceful out there. I just think. It's a form of meditating."

"I guess you might need it after working in a casino all night."

He nodded. "It can be chaotic."

"You've always been a blackjack dealer?"

"The last five years or so."

"Lots of regulars, I bet."

He shook his head. "Too many, if you ask me."

"So, you must know Phil Gabelli then."

"What does he look like?"

I pulled out a picture and handed it to Blake.

"Maybe."

Another hedge. "Is that a yes or a no?"

"You know how many people play each day?"

"Surely you must know I can get a court order and check the casino's surveillance."

"But the casino is on Seminole territory. They have their own police."

So that was his angle. "Let's say we have a memorandum of understanding. Now, how well do you know Phil Gabelli?"

"If it's the same guy I'm thinking, he came in about once a week or so."

"Once a week, over five years, you'd get to know a guy."

"You know how many tables of blackjack we have?"

I did. It wasn't many. "Was he a good player?"

"I don't remember."

Blake kept dancing around for fifteen minutes. I knew he was hiding something, but I moved on.

"You know, I always wanted to learn how to sail."

"You should try it. It's very relaxing."

"Is the Sunfish a good boat?"

"It's pretty nice, but the best thing about it is it's mobile."

"Sounds perfect. Hey, would you mind showing me yours?"

"I'd love to, but I sold it."

"Interesting. When was that?"

"What's so interesting about that?"

"You just said it was a good little boat, and here you go and sell it."

"I'm getting something bigger, if that's all right with you."

"When did you get rid of it?"

"I sold it about ten days ago."

"Like I said, I'm interested in learning to sail. Who'd you sell it to?"

36

LUCA

IT WAS ONLY FIVE-FORTY, BUT I GOT OUT OF BED KNOWING I'd never fall back to sleep after an unsettling dream about Vargas. Well, at least it wasn't another Barrow-case nightmare. I was anxious to follow up on Blake and his boat, but I was due in court at nine. The Russian car theft ring trial had been postponed, waiting on my testimony, and was finally on the calendar. With almost two hours to kill, I decided to take a walk on the beach to get some physical and mental exercise in.

As my feet hit the sand by the Turtle Club, the day I met Kayla hit me with mixed emotions. I'd had Kayla's number for two weeks now and hadn't called her yet. I didn't know what was fueling the procrastination, my lingering, male plumbing issue, or the fear she wouldn't prove to be as interested as I seemed to be. It was getting stupid, I thought, and right there and then I resolved to call her that night.

BLAKE'S STORY on the Sunfish checked out. The guy down at Lowe's Marina confirmed he bought Blake's boat two weeks ago. It was still on his lot, and I asked him to take it off the market and move it indoors. He objected, but when I told him it would only be for a week or so, he agreed and took me to see the craft.

I walked around the white fiberglass skiff. Peering into a kayak-like opening, I noted it accommodated a sailor's legs. There weren't any signs of blood, but I wasn't expecting any. I spied a back support that covered a small storage area. When it was removed it increased the size of the cavity. It'd be a tight fit to sneak a man the size of Gabelli into it, but it wasn't impossible.

Staring at the boat, I tried to visualize how it looked now versus the night Blake was at Clam Pass. After a minute of imagining, I took some pictures and made sure the sales guy removed the *For Sale* sign before heading to Immokalee.

LEAVING THE CASINO, I was feeling good about my persistence on Blake and his job. Rather than giving up when his fellow dealers gave me nothing, I moved on to a couple of cocktail waitresses and hit pay dirt with one of them. In all honesty, it was the natural angle, given the playboy Gabelli was, but it still provided a needed boost to my confidence.

Nancy, a big-boned server, never would have made it past the first interview in the old days. According to an unspoken code, that also guided stewardesses, Nancy didn't have it in the looks department. The brunette, who served drinks in the blackjack section, had so many piercings she looked like she'd fallen into a tackle box.

The one that got me was the tongue piercing. Every time

she opened her mouth I wondered if the ornamentation was painful. No matter how much anyone drank, you had to be deranged to think it was sexy. Anyway, she knew Gabelli right off the bat and said he was hot. I refrained from telling her more because I don't like to talk about the dead.

I asked her what she could tell me about Gabelli, but other than being a flirt and a big tipper there was nothing revealing. That is until I asked about Blake and him, then gold flowed out of her ornamented mouth. I was so excited I almost forgot to ask about Stewart. The cocktail waitress said he rarely came in with Stewart, which I found surprising.

A ton of traffic crawled on Immokalee, and I was tempted to use my siren to speed the ride to see Blake.

"HE WAS A JERK, okay? A big mouth."

Blake's anger flush took on a weird hue over his deep tan. No doubt Gabelli riled him up, the question begging to be answered was whether the riling moved to irrationality.

I said, "You're not the first person to tell me that. He was a piece of work, huh?"

"I know it's not all of them, but these pretty boys, they think everyone's got to kiss their ass. You know what I mean?"

As a quasi-member of that club, I didn't agree but wanted the venom to flow. "And how. What kinda things did he do?"

"He was a medium player, not a real high roller, but he always called over to the pit bosses and talked like he owned half the place. He was always asking for something."

"You mean like a break or something?"

"No, little penny-ante things, like lozenges, aspirin, a

cookie, you name it, he asked for it, and got it. It's like he wanted to show everybody that he was being catered to."

"He really got under your skin, didn't he?"

"Yeah, I hated when he sat at my table. And you know, he knew I didn't like him, and he'd push my buttons and keep pushing all night."

"So that night you lost it?"

"He kept holding the cards when the hand was over. You can't do that. I had to call the pit boss over twice, and he tried to make it like I was picking on him. Then he did it again and I yelled at him to give me the cards. And that scumbag Perez, he sided with Gabelli. It was embarrassing."

"Customer's always right."

"No, that's bullshit. I can't tell you how many times people are thrown out of the casino. We're trained to death about maintaining order."

"But they let Gabelli off the hook?"

"Like I said, the bastard had a way about him."

"What a weasel. I heard you confronted him later."

"They took me off the floor, and I spent the rest of my shift at the cashier's window. When I left to go home, he was outside hanging around. It was like, what, is this guy stalking me? I walked past him to the employee garage, and he just kept busting my balls. So, I got in his face, and another dealer had to separate us."

"Wow. He must've been going nuts."

"I'm not proud of it. I nearly lost my job, had to beg my manager because of that shithead."

"So, you got back at him by putting him in Clam Pass?"

"Oh no, man. I had nothing to do with any of that."

"Yeah, well you were at Clam Pass the night he went missing, and his body was found weighed down in the water there."

"I told you I went sailing. I swear that's all. I don't know nothing about what happened to this guy."

"How come you never told me you had a fight with Gabelli?"

"Look, I hated the guy, but that doesn't mean I'd kill him. What kinda guy you think I am?"

"That's what I'm trying to figure out."

37

LUCA

On the way back, I called Vargas. She asked, "How'd it go?"

"This guy is either an incredible actor or he's telling the truth."

"What happened with the boat?"

"That's why I'm calling. Get Finley to authorize a seizure notice and get that Sunfish to the lab."

"You saw something?"

"Nah, it was clean, but unless Blake bleached it, forensics will get something if it's there."

"It's at Lowe's, right?"

"Yeah, the guy's name is Sammy. I gotta run."

"Hold on a sec."

"What's up?"

"I just got a call from the sex crimes unit. Last week they picked up this guy Steven Foster. Seems he was a Boy Scout scoutmaster or something, and a kid, well, he's not a kid anymore, came forward and filed a complaint against him for sexual assaults that happened more than ten years ago."

"Poor kid, but what's that got to do with us?"

"This pervert Foster, well, he said it wasn't him, but he fingered Phil Gabelli as the guy who did it."

My wheels bounced off the curb. "What?"

"I had the same reaction, but I checked with the Boy Scout local, and guess what?"

"Come on, Vargas!"

"Gabelli was Foster's assistant when the assaults took place. I checked with the Boy Scouts, and Gabelli was there when Foster was."

"Holy shit! That could be the reason he took off."

"Thought the same thing. Maybe he knew this was coming out."

"I'm coming straight in. We need to talk to this Foster guy."

Feeling like I'd been shot up with three cups of espresso, I hit the siren and popped the light on my roof.

I ASKED, "What's this guy do that he can afford to live in Tiburon?"

My partner said, "Teacher at Baron Collier High."

"Just great, this clown's around kids all the time."

"I thought there were all price points in Tiburon."

"It's the fees, Vargas. The fees are sky-high," I said as I turned into the development.

The entrance to Tiburon was one of my favorites: a long driveway lined with majestic royal palm trees that reached into a cloudless, blue sky. The community was anchored by the Ritz Carlton Golf Resort, making Naples the only place with two Ritz Carltons. Tiburon had two world-class golf courses, a good location, and homes ranging from five million down to five hundred thousand.

Steven Foster lived on the second floor of a cluster of coach homes called Castillo. If I remembered correctly, they were trading in the seven hundred thousand range. Still a lot of dough on a teacher's salary. When I saw the tiny size of the elevator, I told Vargas we'd have to take the stairs.

I know better than to think I can tell who's a pedophile by looking at him, but a barefooted Foster fit the bill. He was balding, and whatever hair he had left was dyed shoe-polish black. His eyes were definitely beady and he had a flabby belly. But unless the victim was blind, he'd never confuse Gabelli and this cretin.

Foster grabbed the doorframe when we announced ourselves and said, "Homicide?"

"Yes, we'd like to ask you a couple of questions."

"Uh, sure, but I don't know anything about any murders. Please don't tell me they're also saying I killed someone."

He stepped to the side and we entered. The whole place was floored in white tiles that were too small and laid in a diagonal pattern. It's supposed to make a room look bigger, but I could never figure out how. It was a bright place that I didn't think a sleazebag like Foster would like living in. A trio of sliders leading to a lanai let the light and golf course view in.

As soon as we sat around a glass-topped kitchen table, I said, "I'm going to get right to it, Mr. Foster. The charges against you are about as serious as they get. I understand you claimed the accuser had made a mistake and that this was a case of mistaken identity."

"That's the truth, I swear."

Vargas said, "You claimed that the true perpetrator was a man named Phil Gabelli."

He shook his head. "Yes, that's right, it was Phil. He did whatever that kid said happened."

I said, "I understand you and Mr. Gabelli knew each other through the Boy Scouts."

"We led the same troop. I was the scoutmaster and he was the assistant. He seemed like a good guy, but I guess he deserved what happened to him."

I said, "And what was that?"

"I read the papers. I saw that they found him in Clam Pass. He was murdered."

Vargas said, "Who do you think would murder Mr. Gabelli?"

"I don't know exactly, but I guess anyone he, uh, messed around with would have good reason."

Vargas said, "Do you know anybody in particular?"

"I didn't really know him that well."

I said, "But you worked together for, what, three years?"

"Something like that."

I said, "So how did you know that it was Mr. Gabelli who did it then?"

He tilted his head. "I just got this feeling, you know, he was kinda off. You know what I mean?"

Vargas said, "No, tell us."

"I couldn't put my finger on it, but, I don't know, it was the way he looked at the boys. Something wasn't right."

Vargas said, "Yet you let him work for three years with the boys you were responsible for."

"I, I, believe me, I feel a heavy burden of responsibility for what happened."

I had no worries about how this guy felt, and said, "You don't look anything like Phil Gabelli, who was a fit, good-looking guy."

Foster sucked his gut in and said, "Maybe I haven't aged as good as the next guy, but I'm telling you, we were almost look-alikes."

With an obvious smirk, I said, "If you say so."

Foster rose, "Hold on a sec."

Vargas and I exchanged glances as Foster rummaged through a whitewashed credenza.

"Here, see, what did I tell you?"

I took the picture he held and did a double take. It was Foster, maybe ten, fifteen years ago in his Boy Scout uniform. He looked totally different, but I didn't see much resemblance to the pictures I'd seen of Gabelli. I tried to read into the photo. The silly, yellow ascot thing he had on didn't help. Anybody wearing that would look strange.

"When was this taken?"

"Not sure exactly, but I'd say a dozen years ago. So, you believe me now?"

"Can we have the picture?"

"Sure, if it helps to clear me."

38

LUCA

TWO WEEKS AFTER THE AUTOPSY, A CHIME ANNOUNCING AN e-mail sounded. It was from the crime lab. Opening it, I read the Gabelli toxicology report. I couldn't believe my eyes. There was nothing found but an alcohol reading. I didn't understand some of the medical lingo, so I dialed Bosco's number.

"Doc, it's Frank. I got the Gabelli toxicology. He's the one we pulled out of Clam Pass."

"Yes. I'm familiar with the case. What about it?"

"It says there was no evidence of any illicit drugs in his system."

"Yes, that's correct."

"That's impossible. You said so yourself."

"Not quite. What I said was that drugs may have played a role as the victim had no evidence of heart disease."

"Then there had to be something."

"Afraid not, Frank. There wasn't anything other than an alcohol level that, if I recall, was borderline legal."

"It doesn't make sense. I was sure they'd come up with something. They checked for all substances?"

"It's standard practice, and keep in mind we also checked for prescription drugs, like opioids, barbiturates, and amphetamines."

"So, it was a heart attack?"

"It appears to be."

"Tell me, Doc, if this guy died naturally of a heart attack, like you're saying, why would somebody try to hide the body or make it look like he disappeared?"

"Isn't that your area of expertise, Detective?"

I DIDN'T GET IT. Why make it look like murder? What the hell was going on? A heart attack in a healthy male? Wait, there was that crazy case where that woman was put on trial for killing a guy with sex. She'd given the old bastard a heart attack. Gabelli certainly liked the girls. Could it be something like that? But why cover it up? If his heart gave out making whoopee it wasn't a crime. Unless there was some facet to it that caused his heart to blow.

Could someone have hired a sex tigress to give him a heart attack, using one of the popper things that race your heart? After he collapsed they panicked, or, who knows, maybe they started arguing and wanted to get rid of the body? But what was there to gain? You kill someone out of jealousy, for love, for money, for revenge. What's missing is a reasonable motive.

I punched in a number into my cell.

"Doc, it's me again. Say, I've been thinking about Gabelli and his heart attack. Could it be that he was using or someone gave him a popper during sex?"

"You mean Amyl Nitrite?"

"Yeah, that's it."

"Amyl Nitrite is a vasodilator; it causes the blood vessels to dilate. As a result, the user's blood pressure drops quickly, while at the same time the drug causes the heart to race."

"Sounds dangerous."

"Like all drugs, it is."

"Could it have caused Gabelli's heart attack?"

"Difficult to say. There've been cases of cardiac arrest with its use. But usually it's a habitual use thing that over time weakens the heart muscles."

"Did you check for it in the toxicology workup?"

"No, it's extremely difficult to pinpoint it as it dissipates very quickly. We could try running a test and see what comes back, but I didn't see any evidence the victim was a user."

"How could you tell if he was using?"

"Typically, small crusty, yellow lesions are found around the nose and mouth. The nasal cavities are also inflamed."

"You said his nose was inflamed. Remember?"

"Yes, but it's my opinion that Amyl Nitrite was not the cause. Like I said a moment ago, if it were, there would be signs of use."

"Can you do me a favor? Run whatever report you need to see if you can find any traces of Amyl Nitrite."

"If you insist, Frank. I'm heading to the Keys tonight for a week. I'll do it when I get back."

"Can't you get to it before you head out?"

"I've got that six-month-old baby who died, that the parents say was sudden death syndrome, to autopsy, as well as an eighteen-year-old who overdosed. Therefore no, I can't."

"I hear you, Doc. Have a good time. Just promise me you'll do it as soon as you get back."

THE MORE I thought about it the more frustrated I became. How did Gabelli really die? Was it just a heart attack? If that was it, what the fuck was he doing submerged at Clam Pass? If it was murder, then dumping the body is normal. But If it was a natural death, why was he dumped, and who was responsible for it?

AS I HEADED into the office I knew the Gabelli riddle had to be put on hold at least until we got the advanced blood work back. Vargas and I had no other active case besides Gabelli, and we'd hit a wall. It'd take at least a week after the doctor ordered the extra toxicology workup to come in. We had two boring weeks ahead of us. If I hadn't already used up all my time recovering, it would be a perfect time to take a vacation.

That made it time to do what I hated, going through cold cases. I know some detectives love the opportunity to uncover a fellow officer's mistakes or omissions and solve a dusty case. But to me, and I know it sounds strange, I'd rather leave a sleeping bear alone. It was just more evidence of how flawed we are, and I certainly didn't need any more reminders.

Knowing I would be putting in time on old cases was the only thing that made me hesitate taking the job down here. Reviewing cold cases was boring and time-consuming. Interviewing people years later, whose memories and recollections were muddied by time, took a great deal of patience, a trait I was currently low on.

I couldn't understand why Kayla hadn't called me back. I

had called that night and left a message. Waiting for the call-back was adding to my frustration. If she didn't call me back in a day, I'd try one more time and then, well, let's see what happens.

39

LUCA

ROBIN WAS REALLY UNNERVED WHEN I TOLD HER WHAT WAS going on. She swore up and down it was a vicious lie. I wanted no part of the emotion, I just wanted an old photo of her husband. After six requests, she finally paused her venting and got me a picture. It was a good one, nice and sharp. I assured her I'd get the mess cleared up, keeping it out of the papers, and said goodbye. Getting into my car, a text alert from forensics said that the report on Blake's boat was ready.

Putting the phone away, I held the pictures of Gabelli and Foster side by side. They had similar builds, but Gabelli was at least two inches taller, according to the DMV. Foster's hair was also darker and a lot shorter than Gabelli's was. It wasn't the time between haircuts. If anything, Gabelli's, though longer, appeared recently trimmed.

I put the Gabelli photo on the dashboard and took a closer look at Foster. His beady eyes stared right back at me. This guy was creepy, but if they were both wearing those blue Boy Scout uniforms, could a kid mistake Gabelli for him?

It was tough for me to buy the mistaken identity thing. I

could tell they were very different people, even though I'd never met Gabelli. Foster was mousy, and everything I learned about Gabelli classified him as an overconfident extrovert. My gut was telling me Foster was looking to pin a crime on a dead man. But I couldn't discount it, much as I wanted to.

No matter who it was, though, there was a killer still out there. To focus the hunt for the murderer I'd need to know if it was an abuse-revenge thing or not.

I called Vargas, asking her to get behind the wheel of the backhoe and start digging immediately. I had a doctor's appointment in the morning and wanted to get to the forensic lab before they closed.

IT WAS RAINING SO HARD I waited in my car for more than ten minutes. As soon as it slowed, I jumped out and puddle hopped my way into work.

Speckled with wet spots, I fanned my shirt as Vargas finished up a call.

"Get anything on Foster?"

She frowned. "Good morning, Frank. How did your doctor visit go?"

I exhaled. "Morning, Vargas. Everything's hunky-dory, okay? Can we talk shop?"

"Are you sure?"

"Yes, Mommy. I'm gonna be around awhile. You have anything?"

She nodded. "Foster moved down here sixteen years ago. He was born in Minnesota and taught in Hermantown, a suburb of Duluth, for close to a dozen years before resigning. I didn't like the way the administrator said he resigned, and I remember my sister saying you usually need twelve years to be vested in a school pension. When I mentioned that it was strange he'd walk away so close, she agreed. It was the way she agreed; I knew she was holding back. So, I called the Hermantown PTA and tracked down the president during the time, a guy named Joe Saturn."

"Get to it, Vargas. I'm dying of suspense."

"Saturn said a parent had complained that Foster had acted inappropriately with their son. Something about being in a closet with the seven-year-old."

"Scumbag. What happened?"

"He said it was never pursued further because the parents of the child didn't want to have their kid stigmatized, and there were no other witnesses."

"They let it go?"

"Afraid so, but SCU found a ton of child porn on his laptop, so Foster's gonna be a guest of the State of Florida for a long time."

"He should be hung."

"Maybe. What about the boat?"

"Zippo. No blood or fibers. Nothing. Neighbors also verified that Blake was always going sailing in the middle of the night."

"Blake is clean?"

"Seems to be."

"We back to square one?"

I didn't need the reminder. Every investigation has a ton of dead ends, but I was getting tired of chasing ghosts in this one.

I said, "I got to call Robin and tell her that her husband was just being used by that creep Foster."

40

LUCA

Tired after another fitful night's sleep, I slipped a disc in, put my elbows on the desk, and hit fast-forward. When I found the spot where Blake and his boat appeared I resumed normal viewing speed. The grayness rolled by, but there was nothing of note as the first of the beach walkers came into the lot. It made no sense to pay as close attention to the day visitors since it was now the second day he was missing. Even speeding the video up, it was taking a ton of time. Before I knew it, my pee alarm went off and I took a potty break.

The parking lot grayed with the onset of dusk and I eased the tape back to normal speed. At 8:09 a dark-colored Audi A6 came into the lot, catching my attention with its weaving. A drunk? It pulled close to the entrance and parked. Fifteen minutes passed and then the driver's door opened. I had my eyes on the bald man who emerged when the passenger door swung open and a long-haired woman in slacks came out waving to her man. Baldy, who didn't appear inebriated, walked over to her. They linked arms and disappeared down the boardwalk.

The couple came back from their walk at 9:23 and drove off. Shortly afterward, one of those tiny Fiats came in the lot. Sure enough, it was a young couple who got out and began necking. They retreated into their car and left the lot when a Lincoln SUV came into the lot at 10:37. I watched the Lincoln start to bounce gently at 11:05, and they had their fun until leaving at 12:21.

The parking lot was quiet until 2:08, when one of the ugliest cars ever made, a Nissan Cube, came into the lot. The white Cube drove slowly into the lot as I struggled to see if anyone other than the driver was in it. I paused the tape. It looked like it was a male wearing a baseball cap driving, but I still couldn't tell if he was alone.

The Cube headed for the left corner of the lot and disappeared from the tape, out of the camera's view. The time stamp on the video kept rolling, but there was nothing to see. I was begging for something to pop out of the grayness. Finally, at 2:41, the Cube came back into view and headed out the lot. I slowed the video as the passenger side came into view. It looked like someone or something could be in the passenger seat, but it was impossible to tell.

I rewound the video to get the license plate number as the Cube came in. The damn plate wasn't readable. I stopped the tape and zoomed in. All I could get was the last three: 7KW. I jotted it down and moved on.

The herky-jerky video showed nothing until 4:28 a.m., when a white or maybe silver Ford Focus came in, parking close to the entrance. A guy I figured in his thirties got out, leaned on his car, and lit a cigarette. He took a couple of drags and flicked it into the brush. What's the matter with people? I wanted to ring the moron's neck as he drove off.

Soon the lot was awash in daylight and a parade of walkers and sun worshippers began streaming in with their paraphernalia. The lot emptied as I fast-forwarded to a 5:00 p.m. time stamp and paused it to go to the bathroom.

I made another call to Kayla but was greeted by her answering machine. After leaving a message, I grabbed a coffee and bagel from the kitchen and sat back at my desk. At ten, the lovers started to drip into Clam Pass. Some took walks, and others, well, who knew what was going on inside those cars? There were always two cars in the lot until 1:09, when it emptied. At 2:31 one of those Chrysler PT Cruisers came in.

It didn't pull in head-on but instead parked across a couple of spots near the entrance. Two guys got out and opened its hatchback. I inched toward the screen as they dragged out what looked like a large black plastic bag. The men carried the bag, which appeared heavy, and headed down the boardwalk.

What the hell was in that bag? What was the color of the wrapping they found Gabelli in?

I rewound the tape and made a note of the license plate, which was visible as they came in, and grabbed the case file. Thumbing through, I confirmed Gabelli had been wrapped in black plastic. What threw me off was that there were two men. Usually, when more than one person is involved in a killing it involves organized crime or gangs. We'd seen no evidence Gabelli's bookies had anything to do with his disappearance, but had we cleared them too quickly? Was this another one of my slipups?

41

LUCA

SIPPING A COFFEE, I HEADED TO MY OFFICE FEELING LIKE warmed-over dog doo. It was four days running I'd slept like shit. The nightmares had returned after an unusually long hiatus that I'd been grateful for. I'd been dogged by nightmares involving the Barrow kid, but they came never more than once every couple of weeks and never on consecutive days. Why the sudden ramp-up? Getting cancer, peeing like a girl, and having to take Viagra ain't enough?

Making things even spookier was a disturbing new twist. Now the unsettling visions starred me in the third person.

In the past, almost every Barrow nightmare I suffered through featured the Barrow kid hanging from all sorts of places. Most often he was suspended in his jail cell, but he also showed up in my closet, the garage, the refrigerator, even my office. It had always been the same: Barrow twisting ever so slightly, feet pointed due south, chin on chest, shoulders slumped with his eyes wide open, boring holes in me.

The new iteration that kept me from sleeping had two versions. In the first one I was lying in a hospital bed with the drapes drawn. A pair of doctors came in and told me my cancer had come back and that I had just days left to live. When I tried to ask questions, they opened the drapes, revealing a giant-sized Barrow hanging from exposed pipes. The oversized Barrow was shrieking that he'd finally gotten his revenge on me.

Even scarier was the one I'd had the last two nights. In those nightmares, I went to my oncologist's office for an urgent visit but I couldn't get in because the waiting room was filled with dozens of Barrows hanging from the ceiling. Frightened I'd miss my appointment, I began banging into the bodies, snaking my way through the hanging corpses into a stark examination room. There was nowhere to sit or be examined and I started to panic. I tried to leave but the door disappeared when I grabbed the doorknob. When I slumped to the ground, a doctor appeared, telling me the cancer had spread. When I asked the doctor what could be done, he shook his head and pointed. A door materialized. The doctor ushered me through it, into a room filled with empty coffins. When he asked which one I would like, each of the coffins had me laid out naked in them.

I had to find a way to shake these, I thought, as I nodded at Vargas and sat.

"You look terrible, Frank."

"Thanks."

"What's the matter?"

"Nothing."

"Don't tell me nothing. What's going on?"

"Having trouble sleeping, that's all."

"Too much on your mind?"

"Just having some crazy dreams."

"Tell me. My grandmother was Greek. She taught me quite a bit about how to interpret a dream."

00

"They don't mean anything. It's just random things being crunched together."

She shook her head. "Couldn't be further from the truth."

"Come on, Vargas, that's hocus-pocus. Tell me why, then, say you see someone in passing that you hadn't seen in a while, but you get distracted and forget about them. Sure enough, they're in your dream that night."

"There's two different types of dreams. Everybody has that happen. What you're experiencing, the repeated, disturbing nightmares, is totally different. Something's triggering them."

Was she right? "So, you're a shrink now?"

"I'm just trying to help you get some sleep, that's all. Why don't we go through it?"

I stared silently and took a sip of java.

"Come on, what do you say, Frank? It can't hurt."

She should only know. The Barrow stuff did hurt. I didn't know what to do. She was a good listener, but she was also into silly things like horoscopes. Besides JJ, I never said anything to anybody. JJ and I were buds. We shared things guys wouldn't, and not a drop ever leaked out.

But Vargas knew how to keep her mouth shut. She'd proven that, and she really gave a damn about me. I considered her a true friend. I know it's twisted, but the fact is most guys ain't friends with women. They're generally looking to hop in the sack with them. At times, Vargas was attractive physically, but the more I knew her, the more I appreciated what a good person she was.

When I got hit with the cancer. Vargas was genuine in her concern and didn't dish out the macho crap most cops do when a fellow officer is in trouble.

"Hey, Frank, you in there?"

"Uh, sorry, was just thinking."

Vargas rolled her chair over to my desk.

I said, "Not now, Mary Ann."

"Are you sure, Frank?"

"Yeah."

"You got to get it off your chest."

"I know. Look, we'll talk about it another time. Okay?"

"Your call. Frank, I'm not the one getting nightmares."

I HUNG up the phone and leaned back in my chair shaking my head. Not only was I physically exhausted, but I was tired of hitting brick walls. The PT Cruiser lead turned out to be nothing more than two do-gooders camping out at the beach to protect sea turtle nests. I'm telling you, I got nothing against turtles, and I think the effort to protect their nests is a good one. In fact, I think baby turtles are cute. However, we seem to be going a little too far interfering to be sure they make it into the gulf before some bird grabs them as dinner. What about the birds? Don't they have to eat?

Maybe this case just isn't gonna be resolved. Maybe twenty years from today a bored Collier County detective will eat up his day by poring over this cold case. It was seeming likely, and it pissed me off. A break seemed in order.

Stepping away seemed to work for me. Not all the time, but sometimes, things hit you when you're not knee-deep in a case. Time for this detective to dust off an old case.

I got up and dragged a box of files over, running my hand over the archives. Eeny, meeny, miny, moe. I pulled one out and started reading.

Halfway through the papers documenting the investigation into the murder of a Boris Laskin, an intern knocked on the door and handed me a report.

It was the DMV license plate report I'd requested on the Cube. I plopped it into the in-basket and got back to the Laskin case. A reference in the case to a stolen car made me stop and I grabbed the DMV report.

Two pages of plate numbers, and who they were registered to, surprised me. That many people wanted a Cube? And in white? Maybe they limited the color choices. This would require a ton of follow up. Maybe we could get the uniforms to run them down. I flipped the first page over and my heart began to race.

42

STEWART

"Risks must be taken, because the greatest hazard in life is to risk nothing." - Leo Buscaglia

I SAW HIM FROM THE KITCHEN WINDOW; IT WAS THAT DAMN detective again. Heading down the stairs, I pulled my inhaler out, took a hit, and opened the door.

"Oh, hello, Detective Luca. What I can do for you?"

"I've got a couple of questions for you. May I come in?"

Hell no, you can't come in. "Sure."

He sat in the same chair as the first time he came, but this time I wasn't offering him anything. It doesn't pay to be nice to these guys.

"Do you own a white, 2010 Nissan Cube?"

"Nope."

The detective drew a document out of his pocket and unfolded it. "Really? Well here's a copy of the registration."

"I used to own one, but I sold it."

"Now's not the time to be playing games, Mr. Stewart."

Screw you, Luca, you said do I 'own' one. "Perhaps you should be clearer when questioning."

The detective wasn't happy. He stared at me for a bit too long, then he said, "You go down to Clam Pass often?"

"I like the beach there, but I don't go as much as I would like. Besides, I think Vanderbilt's nicer."

"You mean at night?"

"I don't know what you're talking about, Detective."

The bastard dug into his pocket again. What was he, a magician?

"Here's a photo of you in your Cube driving into Clam Pass in the middle of the night on May first."

I looked at the gray, grainy picture and said, "Is that against the law?"

"No, but it lines up nicely with the day that your best friend went missing."

I smiled. "Oh, I get it, so now you think I must've taken Phil's body there and dumped my best bud in the water."

"What were you doing there that night?"

"It wasn't me. I lent my car to a neighbor."

Luca threw his head back and snickered. The smug son of a gun said, "And how is it you recall that?"

"It's easy, Detective Luca, it's the night my best friend in the whole world disappeared. I have a crystal-clear recollection of that night."

"I see. And who is the neighbor you say you lent the car to?"

"I didn't just *say*, I *did* let him use my car. Lenny Nership, he lives just across the street. You can go and ask him."

"Believe me, I will."

Man, I was really starting to hate this guy. "Be my guest."

"What's his address?"

"I don't know, but it's not the one directly across from me but the one to the left. He's the lower unit."

"Why'd you sell the car?"

"What, selling a car's a crime these days?"

"Did you trade it in or sell it privately?"

"Traded it."

"Where?"

"You can save yourself a lot of time by just going to see Lenny."

"Where was it traded in?"

This Luca was anal and getting on my nerves real fast. I was thinking of giving him a Lexus dealer or something to jerk him around, but said, "Germain Honda, down on Davis."

The detective made a note. He looked like he was about to ask another question, but he stood, jammed the notebook in his pocket, and said, "That'll be all for now."

I watched him through the window. Sure enough, he made a beeline to Lenny's place. I knew Lenny wasn't home and smiled at the thought that Luca would have to make another trip. The next time he comes around I'm not going to answer the door. What did being so available get me anyway?

EARLY THE NEXT MORNING, Lenny texted me and said that Luca had just left. Said the detective wanted to know if he borrowed my Cube and that he told him yes. When Luca asked him why, he said he had a date and that his car was a junker. And that was the end of that.

I hoped Luca would leave me alone now.

43

LUCA

V<small>ARGAS</small> <small>TOOK</small> <small>ONE</small> <small>LOOK</small> <small>AT</small> <small>ME</small> <small>AND</small> <small>SAID</small>, "W<small>HAT</small> happened?"

I shook my head. "I really thought we'd tie Stewart to Clam Pass. But it seems he lent his car to a neighbor."

"Really?"

"Yeah, the neighbor had a date and his car's a junker, so he used Stewart's Cube."

"Date part going to Clam Pass at night makes sense."

"I know, the guy was a little off, though."

"You think he was lying?"

"No, no. I mean he was just kinda weird, I don't know, like a touch of autism or something."

"What? Now you can diagnosis autism?"

"No, I don't know what else to call it. He was the kinda guy who'd have his car covered in stickers. You know what I mean?"

Vargas shook her head. "You know, Frank, anybody else would think you're crazy."

"Me? You're the one who believes in stuff like horoscopes."

"Don't get so defensive, Frank. I was trying to say that I did understand what you meant by the sticker reference."

"You did?"

"You're wound too tight, partner. You still not sleeping?"

I nodded.

"I think I can help if you just open up a little."

I nodded.

"Tell me about the dreams."

Vargas closed the door and I opened up. I told her about the recurring nightmares featuring the hanging Barrow kid and the new twist about me dying.

"They sound terrifying. Tell me about the Barrow case."

I hung my head. "It's embarrassing, Mary Ann. You're not going to like it, but trust me, I learned from it."

"Frank, there's no judging here. I'm your partner and friend."

"It was the first homicide case that I had real input on. It was sort of a high-profile case, as the victim was the niece of a county official. I worked the case with an old-timer, Bob Stone, who was a year away from retiring. I thought it'd be a real learning experience, working with a veteran, but it was almost the complete opposite. This poor girl was strangled with a rope and found in the woods of a park less than a mile from her home. Right away the focus went on the ex-boyfriend, a kid named Dominick Barrow. They'd broken up just two weeks before she was found dead. The girl had ended the year-long relationship, crushing Barrow."

I took a sip of water and continued.

"Given the relationship, I knew the kid was a primary suspect, but Barrow had no record and we had no forensic evidence. We brought the kid in and got nothing other than an admission he was distraught over the relationship. But we did catch him in a lie. He said he'd been nowhere near the park on the day she went missing, but CCTV footage had him walking out of the park. He couldn't explain it and never changed his story. That bothered me, but when I pushed Stone to broaden the search for other suspects it went nowhere. A search of Barrow's house turned up a rope that the medical examiner said could be the murder weapon. The problem for me was there wasn't any forensic evidence to tie it to the body. Stone was adamant, though, said the kid could've cut off the part he used or had bought two ropes."

"Oh boy, sounds flimsy."

"It was, but the brass was pushing for closure, claiming pressure from the Freeholders, that's the name of the town, Freehold, and when a kid came out of nowhere to say that Barrow had recently strangled a stray cat, it was game over for Barrow."

"What happened?"

"I knew we didn't have enough. I felt it was less than circumstantial. Even if the kid did strangle a cat, it's sickening and cruel, but killing another human being is a long leap. Stone wanted to arrest the kid, but I said it was too early and that we needed more. Next thing I know, Stone and the captain, this bastard named Kilihan, they corner me, asking me if I'm a team player or not. What's to lose by arresting him? Maybe he confesses, they say. So, I go against my better judgment and agree to sign off on it." I shook my head and said, "Well, we arrest this poor kid, and the kid hangs himself the first night in custody."

"Oh Jesus."

"I know, it gets worse. Of course, the parents blamed us for the death of their kid, who they said was innocent, and less than three months later someone confesses to the murder."

"That's a tough one, partner."

"Tell me about it."

"It's completely understandable that you are over-whelmed by guilt, but you've got to put it into context. It wasn't your decision alone."

"Yeah, but I could've prevented it."

"Remember you were a rookie, Frank. You didn't have any pull."

"I could've went to the press."

Vargas shook her head. "You wouldn't have done that. You couldn't put your neck that far out. That would've been the end of your career."

"Maybe."

"No maybes. You had a role, a minor one, Frank, but if you didn't go along with it, do you honestly believe they wouldn't have brought the kid in? Cut yourself a break. And while you're at it, don't forget to remember the kid didn't help himself with the misleading alibi."

I shrugged. She had a point, but I had chewed this over and over and over. I said, "But don't you think it was terrible to go along?"

"Let me ask you a question. If nobody confessed to the strangulation, would you feel better about it?"

"Of course."

"But that wouldn't mean this Barrow kid did it, right?"

"But we would've kept investigating."

"Do you really believe that? If the kid was getting framed he wouldn't have a chance."

"Something might have come up."

"You can continue to beat yourself up over it, but that isn't going to change anything. Accept it, you made a mistake, but the reality is, even if you would've tried to buck the pressure, the kid was going to be arrested. No doubt in my mind, and if you're honest with yourself you'd see it as well. It's time to move on, Frank. This was over ten years ago."

"You're probably right."

"You've been through a tremendous amount of stress, Frank. It's completely normal to experience unsettling dreams, but you can help yourself by letting go of this unfortunate case. Promise me you'll try."

I nodded.

Mary Ann said, "Now the vision of your cancer coming back is typical. It's a natural fear, and, though you have a clean bill of health, is completely normal. You had a brush with death, and you would have experienced these visions even without the lingering guilt over the Barrow case. But they wouldn't have been so severe. Somewhere in your mind, you think you should be punished for the Barrow case and that's why you got cancer. Do you understand that, Frank?"

I had to think that through. "It makes sense. I didn't connect the two."

"The cancer you can't control, but the guilt you can. Does that help?"

Something clicked, not a mountain mover, but I understood the logic. "More than you'd think. Thanks, Mary Ann. I really appreciate it."

"Anytime, anytime. Look, I hate to run, but I got to get to court."

MARY ANN WAS SOMETHING. What she said made complete sense; she nailed it. There was no doubt I was going try my hardest to let the Barrow case go. At a minimum, I owed it to myself and to her. She deserved it. I wonder why she never got married. Maybe being a cop pushed away a lot of suitors.

It was a shame. Vargas was a sweet, understanding woman, and she was a pretty good looker as well. She deserved someone who could appreciate her, but there were a lot of whackos out there.

Speaking of whack jobs got me back to Stewart. What an enigma. I thought about my visit with him, which kept bothering me. Even though the car thing panned out, there was no doubt Stewart didn't like seeing me at his door. To be fair, all people, even the most honest Abes, are nervous around cops. But Stewart? I thought I could smell fear coming off him.

He wasn't as neatly dressed as usual, and his place was messy. But I'd come unannounced. Maybe he was like everybody and straightened up only when people were coming around. But the way he had held back information smelled like he was protecting somebody. The likeliest prospect was Robin, but I wasn't seeing her as a killer any longer.

I felt kinda pissed at myself that I'd pushed the theory that she and Phil planned this to collect the insurance money. That theory imploded when Gabelli's swollen body was pulled out of Clam Pass. The conspiracy part went up in smoke, but that didn't mean she had nothing to do with the death of her husband. Her bank account was sitting on three million dollars of motivation. Plus, she had a sack full of marital problems.

44

LUCA

SOMETIMES YOU GOTTA GO AFTER THINGS LIKE CRAZY, AND sometimes they just fall in your lap. I finished the call and hung up the phone.

"You're not gonna believe this, Vargas, but that was Goren."

"Who?"

"The guy who owned that construction firm, Simmons Construction, that Gabelli worked for."

"Oh yeah, he was a creep. He'd nearly drooled when I went to see him."

"Oh, so I've got something in common with him then?"

Vargas smiled, and I thought there was a hint of a blush in her cheeks.

"Anyway, he said they uncovered what he said looked like fraud on a contract that Gabelli was responsible for."

Vargas leaned forward. "They think he was stealing?"

"Looks like that. Goren said Gabelli signed off on a wire for a project they were building in Barbados to a recipient whose name was close enough to pass. They followed the money, and as soon as the wire hit, it was bounced to another bank in Saint Martin before going to a bank in the Caymans, where it disappeared."

"How much we talking?"

"Six hundred K."

"Six hundred thousand is a lot of money. How did it take so long to surface?"

"He said it was a long-term, multi-building project that'd been going on for a couple of years, and when it was over a contractor said there was a balance due."

"Now what?"

"They're doing an audit, but this could be the crack in the egg."

"No doubt."

"Gabelli had good reason to hightail it, especially if they uncover anything else."

Vargas nodded. "Or he was stealing to cover his gambling debts."

"I don't know, could be he covered his losses knowing this would surface and took off before it did."

"Plausible."

I had to agree. "Yeah, definitely in the mix, but I need more info before moving off him taking the dough and splitting, maybe even with another one of his playmates."

"You think he was working the fraud with someone else, and when it came time for them to split the money Gabelli said no?"

I nodded. "Or he gambled the money away. Didn't have it, and he finally got whacked."

My cell buzzed. It was Kayla. I headed outside and answered, "Hello."

"Frank, hi, it's Kayla."

"Hey, how you doing?"

"I'm doing good, but how are you feeling?"

"A hundred and fifty percent. Everything's back to normal."

"That's great. What happened?"

"I had to have some surgery, had a couple of small tumors in my bladder, of all places."

"Oh my God. That must have been scary for you."

"Let's say I didn't need the drama, especially in the middle of my first date with you-know-who."

"I called to check on you, you know."

"Thanks, my partner told me. I wanted to call you, but I didn't have your number, and things were crazy, to say the least."

"But everything's good now?"

"Absolutely. I was out of commission for a couple of months. I was going out of my mind with nothing to do."

"Me, I would've been at the beach every day."

"I went often enough, but, anyway, I had a bit of a time hunting down your number. You'd make a good spy."

It sounded like music when she laughed. "Not really."

"It'd be great to get together again. Besides, I still owe you a dinner. You happen to have any plans to come back down?"

"I'd love to, but at the moment I've been helping out my parents. My dad had one of his lungs removed."

"Sorry to hear. How's he doing?"

"Pretty good now. He had the surgery about four months ago and was doing well but developed a bad infection and had to be hospitalized again. Then he was in rehab for a while, but now he's starting to bounce back."

"Must be tough on your mother."

"It is. My dad did everything, and now Mom is scurrying around trying to cover the bases while working full time."

"Well, you're doing the right thing being there for them."

"I'm really happy to help them. But it's not like I don't want to scream at times." She laughed.

"I'll bet."

We chatted about the weather, her job, and then what cases I was working before we starting winding down the call.

"I used all of my time off and more with the surgery and all, but maybe I'll sneak up and see you for a weekend."

"That'd be nice."

"Great. Maybe in a couple weeks, would that work for you?"

"I'd love it, but let's wait till things settle down with my dad. I hate for you to come up here and I'm tied up with them."

"Sounds like a plan."

45

LUCA

ROBIN DIDN'T SEEM SURPRISED TO SEE US, WHICH LEFT ME wondering as we took seats in swivel chairs. She wasn't flirty this time. Was it because Vargas was around, or had she been toying with me?

She said, "Is there something you have to tell me about Phil?"

Vargas said, "We have some questions to ask you about your husband and the work he was doing."

"His job? What's that got to do with his murder?"

I said, "Did you know that your husband was involved in a scheme, defrauding his employer?"

Her shoulders slumped. "Phil was stealing?"

Vargas said, "You had no knowledge of it?"

"Of course not! I don't understand. What was going on?"

I said, "Phil was managing the Sweet Bay project for Simmons. A large payment he personally requested was made and wired to an account unrelated to the contractor."

"I'm not sure I understand. Why would Simmons wire money to a different party?"

Vargas said, "The money was sent to a Sweet Bay

account, but it had nothing to do with a project he was managing. It seems he, and we believe a coconspirator, set up an account under a name very similar, in this case Sweet Bay LLC versus Sweet Bay Resort."

"How much money are we talking about?"

"Six hundred large," I said.

She gasped, "Six hundred million?"

I said, "No, six hundred thousand."

"Oh, when you said large I thought—"

I countered, "From where I come from, a hundred K is large."

Vargas said, "Not much compared to three million, is it?"

"What's that supposed to mean?"

"Nothing, just bringing up the insurance money."

"That has nothing to do with—"

"Ladies, let's get back to the money, it seems, was stolen by Robin's husband."

"Are you sure Phil was involved?"

I said, "I'm afraid there's no doubt. He ordered the wire. The money didn't stay at the first bank for longer than an eyeblink. Then it bounced to at least three other institutions before disappearing in the Cayman Islands."

"Someone could have made it look like he requested the wire."

I said, "True, but his name was on an account, at the Royal Bank of Scotland in Barbados, I think it was. There aren't any Philip Gabellis in Barbados. And the account was opened remotely from a branch in Fort Myers. That's not a coincidence, ma'am, we call it evidence."

Robin slumped further in her chair but remained silent.

Vargas said, "Do you know about any accounts your husband may have had at a bank or credit union?"

"None that I know of."

I said, "Is there anyone you can think of that may have been involved with your husband on this?"

"I still can't believe he did this, no less anyone helping him."

"We know Phil liked to gamble, and he got himself in a couple of jams, owing the wrong people money."

"All's he had to do was come to me, like he did in the past."

I said, "But didn't you tell Dom Stewart that you were sick of bailing Phil out of his gambling holes?"

"You think I liked throwing my hard-earned money to a bookie to cover his losses? Of course, I was pissed, but that doesn't mean I wouldn't help him."

I said, "Maybe he had the sense you wouldn't. Maybe the bookies were putting pressure on him. Maybe he had nowhere to turn to and the pressure made him steal."

"So, it's my fault?"

Vargas said, "That's not what he's saying."

I asked, "What do you think is more likely, that he stole the money to pay off a gambling debt, or he stole the money and was going to use it to start a new life somewhere else?"

"I don't know what to think anymore. This is crazy: he disappears, is found murdered, and now this? You really think it was him?"

I said, "It sure looks that way."

"Well, I can assure you I had no idea about it and find it hard to believe. There has to be an explanation."

I said, "We're going to keep investigating this."

WE GOT BACK into our car.

"This is some neighborhood, Vargas. You see the white one on the left? That's my favorite."

"The houses are nice, but I don't like it back here."

"Why?"

"I don't know, no sidewalks, and it kinda has an old feel to it."

"You'd make a good agent, maybe when you retire."

"No, thanks."

When we pulled onto Pine Ridge, I said, "I don't know, Vargas. It's not adding up. He steals the money, or so we think."

"How can you say that? His hands are all over this."

"True, so let's say he organizes the scheme. Steals the six hundred K to cover a gambling debt or to run away to some Caribbean island."

"Exactly."

"So how does he end up at the bottom of Clam Pass?"

"He gets the money, pays off his debt, and he pisses off the mob and they crush him."

"Nah. Gabelli's an ATM for them. With numbers like six hundred K they'd get him limos."

"Okay, he gets the money, and someone unrelated to the bookmakers knows about it and that leads to his murder."

"I don't buy the gambling angle. We would've heard something if he was into Fingers for six hundred K. And don't forget, they'd be stalking the missus if the debt was still out there."

"So why did he steal the money?"

"Does the money mean anything?"

"Of course, it does."

"If anything, he was planning to disappear. That kinda fits, as you'd think the theft would surface sooner or later. Unless he had some way of keeping it hidden."

"These things always surface. That's why a lot of firms force people to take two weeks in a row off."

"How about someone else made it look like Gabelli stole the money? How come this suddenly surfaced as soon as Gabelli was in the icebox?"

"Hmmn. That's outside the box, Luca, but I like the reasoning. Makes sense."

Maybe I wasn't turning into mush after all.

I said, "No question the dough is interesting, and I've chased down a lot of sleazebags for a helluva lot less than six hundred big ones, but maybe the money has nothing to do with this."

"But you always say there are no coincidences in crime, that it's called evidence."

"It's nice you pay attention, Vargas, but the money is evidence of theft, not murder."

46

STEWART

"Vision without action is a daydream. Action without vision is a nightmare." - Japanese Proverb

I TOOK ANOTHER HIT FROM MY NEBULIZER.

I don't know what got into me. This bitch was really screwing with my head. I gotta change it up, ditch the original plan. It just burns me up to no end to find out Mr. Office Man stayed over at her house the whole freaking weekend.

I went by, what, ten, twelve times? Every time I did, I got more worked up. Why'd I keep going? If I'd just put it out of my mind, things wouldn't have gotten out of control. I mean, who answers the door without a shirt on? It threw me off, and when Robin came to the door with her shirt half unbuttoned, I really lost it.

This was no good. I was wasting time. My life was ticking away, and I was still sitting in an old coach home. Was it time to heat things up with Melissa? That's what it looked like. But I put a lot of time in this, and there was one more thing I had to try before I moved on.

I WASN'T a dog lover at all. They run around outside and then jump all over your furniture. That's crazy. They can make things dirty, and some people even let them sleep on their bed. No way that's happening under my roof.

Robin, she just loves dogs, always wanted one, but not Phil. You see, me and Phil, we thought the same about a lot of things. That's why we were best buds. Dogs was just another example where we lined up like soldiers.

Phil resisted Robin's attempts to get a dog at least a dozen times that he told me about. She'd especially hit him hard on it when he was on the defensive from straying. Like with kids, Phil didn't want to be tied down any more then he had to.

I started browsing around the Internet, knowing if it had to be a dog, it'd have to be a small one and, for sure, one that didn't shed. Maybe it could be trained to do its business inside so it'd stay clean. That'd be up to Robin, but I'd have to influence it. I settled on a Maltese. Robin liked them, and they did seem to be the cutest to me.

The breeder was way out east, off of Pine Ridge, and had three different Maltese litters to choose from. The tea-cup types were the smallest, but I wasn't going to pay for the upcharge, so I picked out a female white ball of fur that was two weeks old.

It was super delicate and fit in the palm of my hand. By the time I was out of there I had charged over sixteen hundred dollars on two cards, and I still had to buy a crate and other puppy paraphernalia.

I put a plastic sheet and then a towel on the front seat and the puppy went to sleep as I drove. It didn't make a whimper and looked so peaceful. My spirits rose. This was going to be one of my better ideas. I called Robin and told her I had to see her immediately. She pissed me off with her stalling, but she eventually agreed.

HOLDING the puppy up against my stomach, I rang her bell. Robin came to the door wearing pink flip-flops, a Beatles tee shirt, and shorts, but no smile. I raised the puppy up and she said, "Oh my God, she's so cute." She nuzzled the pup and said, "Where'd you get her?"

"I got her from a breeder out east, and she's all yours."

"What?"

"I got her for you. I know you always wanted a dog, but Phil, he wouldn't let you."

She handed me back the pup. "But I, I, can't accept it."

"It's okay, it's a gift from me to you."

"But I don't want a dog."

The puppy started whimpering.

"What do you mean? You always said you wanted one."

"I know, but now's not the time."

"It's the perfect time. It'll be good for you."

"I can't take care of it."

"You always said you wanted a dog, but Phil prevented you from getting one, and now you have one."

"I can't take care of it. Don't forget, Phil had flexibility during the day. He could pop in and take care of her."

"You can do it."

"I don't want to be tied down worrying about a dog. It's not fair to me or to her."

And so, it went. I couldn't figure her resistance out, and

we started arguing. I was sick of trying to do the right thing and having it boomerang. I couldn't see trying to convince her anymore, so, crying pup in palm, I marched off to my car and drove back to return the dog. As a final insult, the breeder charged me a five hundred dollar 'processing' fee to take the puppy back.

47

LUCA

I slept almost the whole night through. It was the first time I could remember doing so in a long time, and I felt fresh as I sipped my morning coffee. I was reading a forensics journal when my phone rang.

"Detective Luca? It's Robin Gabelli."

She was as formal as I'd ever heard her.

"Good morning. What can I do for you?"

"It might be nothing, but it was disturbing. I couldn't sleep last night."

"What's bothering you?"

"Well, last night, it was late, after eleven, and Dom came to my house."

"Stewart?"

"Yes, Dom Stewart."

"Okay, what happened?"

"Well, I had company, a friend was staying over, and Dom started ranting."

"A male friend?"

"Yes."

"Did Stewart assault him?"

"No, I thought for sure he was going to. He started cursing and making threats."

"What kind of threats?"

"That's what I wanted to tell you. He said that he'd kill Michael just like he did the other guy."

"Slow down. Michael, that's your friend who was staying over?"

"Yes, he's a friend from work."

"Stewart never laid a hand on this Michael or you?"

"No. He was just screaming. It was scary, and when he said he'd kill him like he did the other guy I went numb. Do you think he meant Phil? They were friends, it can't be, could it?"

"Sometimes people say things for effect. It doesn't mean it's true."

"No, no, this was different. He was, like evil personified. I'm telling you, I've known him a long time, and he gave me the creeps."

I wanted to say, you mean that guy you once jumped in the sack with now gives you the creeps? But asked, "What did your friend think of the threat?"

"He thinks Dom is totally unstable and is probably the guy who killed Phil."

"What makes him so sure?"

"It's not the first time Dom threatened him."

"You never reported a previous incident."

"I didn't think it was such a big deal at the time. You see, Dom always wanted a relationship with me. I know it's my fault for that one-time thing. But a few months ago, I was out with Michael at Brio in Waterside and Dom saw us, and to say he wasn't happy is an understatement."

"Did he get physical?"

"No, not really. Dom was pissing off at me, and when

Michael asked him to leave us alone, he poked his finger in Michael's chest and said something like he'd wipe the floor with him if he didn't mind his own business."

"How'd it end?"

"One of the valet guys came over and Dom walked away muttering to himself, like a complete nut job."

"It might be time to get a restraining order."

"So that he couldn't come near me?"

"You could try for that, but it'd be easier to at least get one to keep him away from your house."

"Can't you bring him in? He said he killed someone, and it could be Phil."

"We need more than hearsay."

"It's not hearsay. Michael heard it too. We both heard it. If you would have seen him last night you wouldn't be brushing it off."

"I'm not brushing it off, but it's not a crime to say things, even if they're crazy."

"You don't believe he did it?"

"It's not a matter of belief; it's evidence we need."

"But he said he killed someone."

"I understand that, but he could have just been trying to intimidate your friend."

"So that's what you think it was, intimidation?"

I had to get back in control here. "Hold on here, Mrs. Gabelli. At this time, there is no legal basis to haul Stewart in. However, you can rest assured that this information will be taken, as is all information, under consideration. Now, I think you should give serious consideration to getting a restraint order. If you decide to pursue one, I'd be happy to contact the prosecutor's office and provide case details on your behalf."

48

LUCA

FINANCIAL CRIMES WERE SOMETHING I'D WORKED ON A handful of times in New Jersey. All of those Jersey cases targeted the legions of corrupt officials that infest the so-called Garden State. We'd taken down a number of mayors and councilmen, but, like cockroaches, a new generation of replacements came out of the woodwork.

After the lead detectives in Collier's Financial Crimes Unit were rear-ended by a landscaping truck, Vargas and I jumped into their case, which was at a critical juncture. There's an endless amount of big money, and by that, I mean really big money, in Naples. You'd think all that money and the savviness of the people with it would make them immune to being fleeced.

Well, you'd be about as wrong as you could be for two major reasons. The first is greed—it infects even the wealth-iest of us. The other, often underappreciated condition, is what I call the 'insider game,' and it's directly related to ego. Some people have an insatiable need to be on the inside of things, to have connections and access that others don't have.

John Seymour understood this and exploited it to the tune

of fifty million dollars. And he did it in record time. When I read the case file I had to stop myself from admiring him. While the incompetent regulators were watching for the next Madoff, this guy Seymour, who played up his Sacramento origins, was raking in cash to supposedly fund Silicon Valley startups.

The problem was there were zero startups, and so all the investors got was to play cocktail braggadocio for several months. I'm pretty sure that even though the investors didn't receive a financial return on their money, for some the social dividend was more than enough.

That is, as long as news they were swindled didn't leak out. Seymour knew this and deftly used it against the folks who lined up to give him money. It was the reason the fraud went on so long. No one would come forward. They were frightened that word would get out and their reputations would be tainted. Who knows, they might not get invited to the best parties anymore.

However, one person did file a complaint, a feisty old lady named Martha Notingham. She lived in an older estate on the gulf and had given Seymour only, and I say this lightly, two hundred thousand. It was a drop in the bucket for Notingham, but she was miffed he rarely returned her calls. Who knows how long Seymour could have operated his little scam if he'd only sweet-talked her a couple of times?

It was Vargas's idea to have the two of us act as relatives of Notingham, looking to invest alongside her. I played her nephew, and Vargas was my wife. I didn't know if it was that I'd never gone undercover before or that Vargas insisted on holding my hand during the meeting that made it surreal. Either way, it was greed on Seymour's part that made him buy into our little show. It wasn't clear to me if Notingham was being herself or acting her part, but she smelt like

English royalty to me. She was one impressive lady, and there was no doubt she was relishing her role in beating Seymour at his own game.

We turned the documents and wiring instructions Seymour asked us to complete over to the DA. They worked with Florida's Banking Commission and Office of Financial Regulation to develop a prosecutable trail and quickly gave us the go-ahead.

Dreymore, an assistant DA, Vargas, and I settled around a conference table. We hooked up the recording device and I placed the call.

"Hello, Mr. Seymour. This is Jonathan Notingham."

"Hello, Jonathan. It's nice to hear from you."

"As it is to talk with you. We've had the documentation reviewed by our family-office attorney, and though he thought we should change a bit of the language, I believe they're minor modifications, and we're comfortable going ahead with the paperwork as is."

"That's wonderful to hear. I do have to say your timing is excellent. You'll be a part of an exciting opportunity that was just brought to me by a long-time contact in the valley."

"Wonderful. They do say timing is everything."

"It sure is. I'd hate to have you miss out on this one. Will you be wiring the funds soon?"

"I've already instructed our bankers. It's being arranged as we speak, and if this delivers the returns you stated, additional investments will be forthcoming."

"It will, you can count on it."

"Excellent."

"I'm sorry, Mr. Notingham, but I'm running late for an investment meeting with a couple of tech titans. We'll speak soon, and do give my warm regards to your aunt."

I said goodbye and hung up.

Vargas said, "Nice going, Mr. Notingham."

Dreymore said, "She's right, he didn't suspect a thing."

"It's greed, it blinds most people," I said.

Vargas said, "You sure you're able to keep our hands on the money? I would hate to think Seymour's going to outfox us."

Dreymore said, "Don't worry. We've alerted everyone along the chain, and the transfer is flagged. Anywhere the money goes, we'll know. Even if it moves offshore, as we suspect it will."

I said, "What about if it goes to say the Cayman Islands or Isle of Man?"

"It doesn't matter, money haven or not."

"The banks are playing ball?"

"They don't have a choice; they've been served."

I pulled the tape out of the recorder, labelled it, and put it into the case file as Dreymore left.

"Yo, Vargas, want to grab a bite at Chipotle? Catching crooks gives me an appetite."

"Chipotle? Mr. Notingham, a man of your means shouldn't frequent such establishments."

"Forgive me, dear. Shall we visit Nemo's."

"If you're paying, I'm definitely in, that is, as long as we can get in."

"You know what? We deserve it."

I turned my phone back on and there was a voice mail.

"I got a message from Bosco."

"What's he say?"

"The Gabelli tox report came back. He said there was no trace of amyl nitrite, but they found something else."

"What?"

"He didn't say, said to call him."

I called him back, but he was in the midst of an autopsy.

49

LUCA

THE RED LIGHT WAS ON OVER THE DOOR TO THE SUITE USED for examining infectious or burned remains.

Damn, how long was this going to take? I peered through the door's small window. Bosco was hunched over what looked like a burned body, speaking into a microphone as he sliced opened a charcoaled abdomen. I watched as he cut away a specimen and dumped it into a stainless-steel pan shaped like a kidney. It was slow going. I left to find a bathroom and a cup of java.

When I came back, Bosco was pulling the sheet back over the body. He rolled the gurney over to a refrigerated chamber and made a quick call. He peeled his gloves off and began washing his hands so slowly that I banged on the door. He looked over, grabbed a towel and headed over.

"Hiya, Doc."

"I'm sorry, Frank, I don't have time."

"I promise this will be quick."

"You know I don't work on just homicides, don't you, Frank?"

"I know, I'm sorry. It's just that your message left me hanging. You said something showed up. What was it?"

"As I mentioned, there were no traces of amyl nitrite, but I widened the toxicology request and a fair level of terbutaline showed up."

"Terbutaline? What's that?"

"It's a bronchodilator. It assists in opening a person's airways to facilitate breathing. It's prescribed for emphysema and asthma sufferers."

Asthma? A vision of Stewart sucking on his inhaler flooded into my head.

"But as far as we know, Gabelli didn't have any issues with his breathing, right?"

"The victim had no known respiratory issues, and his medical records have no indications he was taking any prescription drugs."

"Is there any other reason why a person would take this stuff?"

The doctor smiled. "The only other use I'm aware of is to delay labor."

"You mean when a woman's giving birth?"

He nodded. "In certain cases of preterm labor, doctors will administer it to delay birth in order to improve the health of a premature baby."

"I never heard of that."

"Sometimes it can delay labor for a couple of days, and that's critical to a premature baby's health. Of course, like all drugs, there are risks, especially for the mother."

"Is there any way you could get high off it?"

"No. In fact, it can cause a heart attack when overused."

"How much of terbutaline would cause a heart attack?"

"That's difficult to say. It would depend on the health and body mass—"

"Come on, Doc, we're talking about Gabelli. How much would be needed to cause him to have a heart attack?"

"I'm not an expert on this medication."

"Gabelli had alcohol in his system. Would that contribute?"

"It couldn't help, but again I'm not very familiar with the interactions."

"Thanks, Doc, really I appreciate it. I gotta run."

I punched a number in my cell.

"Vargas, we got the break we've been waiting for. Bosco, bless his scalpel-wielding tail, ran an extra test, and bingo, some drug used for asthma came up."

"Gabelli had asthma?"

"No, but his buddy Stewart does."

"You think he—"

"It looks like it right now, but we've been chasing whispers and ghosts for so long that I got to try to keep it in check. Look, call our pharma guy and get as much on terbutaline as you can."

"How you spelling that?"

"T-e-r-b-u-t-a-l-i-n-e. I'm on the way in."

I RIPPED off my jacket and tossed it on a chair.

"What do you have, partner?"

Vargas held up a sheet of notes. "Terbutaline opens up the airways to make it easier to breathe. It's generally only prescribed when inhalers don't work. He said it has a lot of side effects and definitely can impact the heart. It makes the heart race, and he said it was believed to weaken hearts, especially in pregnant women."

"What forms does it come in?"

"Injectable and pill form."

"How much would it take to cause an overdose and prompt a heart attack?"

"He didn't want to speculate, but said it's a very dangerous drug and should only be prescribed if there's no relief from inhalers. Get this, he said that a mere five-milligram dose elevates the heart rate by thirty percent."

"Wow, and that's a tiny pill. You should've pressed him."

"I did, Frank. He was noncommittal, so I asked him if someone were given five or ten times the dose, what would happen. He said that the injectable form works super-fast and would push the heart to its limits."

"Stewart could've stabbed Gabelli with a needle."

"Maybe, but he also said mixing it with alcohol would exaggerate the effect, called," Vargas looked at her notes, "peripartum cardiomyopathy. Which could lead to a sudden cardiac arrest, a massive heart attack."

I felt a pinch in my side as I said, "I wonder what Gabelli drank?"

"You okay, Frank?"

"Yeah, why?

"You winced like you just had pain."

"I got a little pinch in my side."

"This the first time?"

I couldn't lie. "Got it two or three times. It's no big deal. What else did he say?"

"Did you tell the doctor, Frank?"

"They said it could just be some scar tissue."

As Vargas stared at me, my side felt like it got skewered. "Ouch." I doubled over.

"That's it, Frank. I'm calling an ambulance. You're going to the hospital."

The pain was searing, but I said, "No. I'll drive there."

"You're in no condition to be driving, mister."

I grabbed my side. "I hope there's nothing wrong. It doesn't feel good, Mary Ann."

"What's the doctor's name who operated on you?"

Vargas called for an ambulance and let my surgeon know. On the ride to the emergency room I couldn't shake the belief my cancer had come back. The pain felt bad, really bad. Seeing the trapdoor opening to take me off life's stage scared me out of my mind. I reached for Vargas's hand, pleased she was in the ambulance.

50

STEWART

"All the breaks you need in life wait within your imagination. Imagination is the workshop of your mind, capable of turning mind energy into accomplishment and wealth." -Napoleon Hill

THE SUN WARMED MY FACE AS I BOUNDED DOWN THE STAIRS. I felt really good this morning and was sleeping a lot better since breaking away from Robin. The decision wasn't easy, but it should have been. The only thing we can't make is time, and I knew you shouldn't waste it. No more making mistakes with that.

The Mustang wasn't a Porsche, but it wouldn't look good to be driving a 911 with a gal whose father owned a couple of Ford dealerships. It certainly wasn't the money; they had plenty. Not as much as Robin after she got the insurance money, but Melissa had no brothers or sisters, so it was a pretty good fit for me.

I didn't know anything about the car business, but that didn't stop Melissa, who was the general manager for all the showrooms, from hiring me as the assistant manager for the

Bonita store. The best part was telling Greely I was sick of his bullshit and then quitting. I couldn't resist taking a few shots at him as I left. It felt good to finally execute that plan.

The first couple of weeks at the Ford place I didn't do much, just getting acquainted with everyone, but it was a busy dealership and I didn't like the hours. They were open from nine to nine, six days a week, and Sundays from eleven to five. That sucked a lot of hours out of whatever allotment anyone got in life. I'd put the hours in now, but in a couple of months I'd lean on Melissa to work on the old man. He wouldn't want to deprive his daughter of a home life, would he?

I had to keep reminding myself to stop comparing Melissa to Robin. The thing with Melissa was I had to play the long game. She didn't have the cash flow that Robin did; I found out she was only making a hundred and ten a year. That didn't go very far, and they were only paying me eighty-five. Her dad was a fit, sixty-six-year-old, so the payoff here was a long way off.

The other thing that bothered me was that even though Melissa had grown up with money, she didn't have Robin's sense of style. In virtually every category, Robin outclassed her. Melissa didn't dress particularly well. I hated the frumpy pantsuits she wore to the dealership. And it bugged me when she'd tell me to wear shorts when we went out to eat.

Oh, there was one more thing: her house. Melissa lived in an old, low-rise building in Park Shore that was painted an embarrassing canary yellow. She said the place was comfortable, convenient, and debt free. You can add, furnished like an eighty-year-old lived there.

I'd have to reevaluate the time line for this relationship. Maybe it'd take me a bit longer than I thought, but if I played my cards right and stuck to the plan, I'd find a way to flourish. First, though, I'd wait another three months and then tell her we should move in together. That way I could get out of my place and cut my expenses. I had diddly-squat as far as equity was concerned, but I'd come out with thirty grand or so to pay off my credit card debt.

Then I'd work on her to upgrade our living quarters. She liked the location? Okay, we could move into one of those new high-rises. It'd be sweet, looking at the gulf shimmer with a cocktail in hand.

51

LUCA

I COULD SEE VARGAS WHISPERING ON A PHONE AS THEY rolled me back in from a test. I gave her a thumbs-up and a huge smile.

"It's just a kidney stone."

"Oh, thank God."

"You're telling me. I thought I was done."

"They going to break it up with ultrasound?"

"Yep. Hopefully, with one treatment it will break up. Either way, I'm gonna get released after they zap it."

"Oh, Frank, I was so scared for you."

"Thanks, Mary Ann, I know what you mean. You know, I really thought the cancer had come back and it was game over."

"We didn't need the drama, did we?"

"I'll say. But thanks for coming with me. It was good you did."

"No thanks necessary. I'm just glad it was nothing serious."

"Not serious, but man, kidney stones are painful as hell."

"I know, my mom had them twice."

I adjusted my gown to cover my legs. "It's freezing in here."

Vargas ripped open another hospital gown and put it on top of the sheet.

"Thanks. So, where were we on the Gabelli med thing?"

"Just rest today. We'll pick it up tomorrow."

"I'm fine, the painkiller worked. We can't waste any more time. We've been working this case for far too long. It's either Stewart stabbed him with a needle, or he crushed up a bunch of pills and dissolved them in whatever Gabelli was drinking."

"It had to be crushed pills."

"Why?"

"First, he'd only get one shot at it. If he hit him with a needle, he'd have to be sure the entire dose got in. There'd probably be a struggle as Gabelli tried to figure out what was happening."

"Unless one vial would be enough. You said the pharmacologist said it would work fast."

"Stewart would have to know what a deadly dose was, and even our guy wouldn't commit to it."

"You're right, but he's got asthma. Maybe he found out from his doctor."

"Hm. Maybe."

"But I agree, it's probably easier and safer to pre-crush a bunch of pills and put 'em in his drink. But do these pills have a taste to them?"

"I don't know."

"Check it out and let me know. But either way, we got to drag Stewart in and get a search warrant for his place."

"Sounds like a plan."

"Now get out of here and get to work."

"You sure you're going to be all right?"

"It's only a kidney stone. I'll be out of here in a couple of hours."

Vargas left and I lay there thinking, make that obsessing, over the Gabelli case. So many pieces of promising information had led nowhere. A lot of that data had pointed at Stewart, but now this asthma drug was the string that could tie them all up.

I had to find out who his doctor was. It was always a delicate thing dealing with the medical profession. Those guys hid behind privacy better than the tech companies. In this case we needed to identify the doctor, then all we wanted from the doctor was to know if and when he prescribed terbutaline. We get that, and Stewart's finished.

We shouldn't have too much of an issue getting a search warrant. We'd probably see something at his house that let us know his doctor's name. Who knows, we may even find some of his weapon of choice during the search.

Things always evened out, and we certainly deserved a break in this case. I had to call Vargas and make sure she included the drug in our warrant and told the DA about the threats Stewart made if he balked at issuing the warrant.

Robin. I felt a bit bad at the way I pushed her off when she told me about the threats that Stewart leveled at one of her lovers. But you know what, she wasn't the straightest with me. Like all type As, she thought she could manage me. That was her first mistake, but in the end, it looked like her only one, unless we could find evidence she was conspiring with Stewart.

I needed to settle on a strategy for interviewing Stewart. He was going to be cagey; we couldn't expect him to crack easily. But I'd find a way to make a tiny fracture and ram my crowbar in. I couldn't wait. It was going to be enjoyable watching Stewart squirm.

—————

VARGAS WAS at her desk when I got to work in the morning.

"How you feeling, Frank?"

"Almost as good as new. They were able to shatter it in one session. I'll have some pain as it passes through, but you know how tough I am."

"Yeah, you're a real superman."

"Any news on the warrant?"

"Esposito said we'd probably have it this afternoon."

"Good, good. Now how we going to play Stewart?"

"Hold on a sec, I thought you'd like to know that Gabelli wasn't a thief, after all."

"I didn't think so. Who stole the money?"

"It was the CFO at Simmons who orchestrated the fraud and made it look like Gabelli."

"No shortage of people looking to pin crimes on the dead."

"And how. Now, back to Stewart."

"We need to figure out how we're going do this. You think we drag Stewart in before the search or after?"

Vargas said, "If we pull him in before, Stewart's going to clean up anything that might raise questions. On the other hand, if we showed up with the warrant before talking to him, he'd really be on guard during an interview afterward."

"I know. But I have enough confidence we'll crack him, even if he's on guard. I think ten minutes in, he'll put his Teflon up."

"We could arrest him first, then talk to him. That might shake him up."

I shook my head. "I don't like it. We might get something we can use early on. We see him, try misdirecting him, maybe he'll spill something. We arrest him, his lawyer's there, and I don't think we have enough to get the DA to sign off on an arrest at this point."

Vargas frowned. "I know everything is circumstantial."

"Unless we find something at his place. Okay, what's our theory about how he killed Gabelli?"

"The two of them got together at Stewart's home. They're watching sports and drinking. Stewart had crushed a dozen or so pills and dumped them into Gabelli's drink."

I said, "You think he put them all in at once?"

"I'd say he puts about ten percent in the first drink. This way it gets into Gabelli's bloodstream, and then he loads the rest in the second one."

"Two drinks would get him to just under the legal limit, right where the autopsy said his blood alcohol level was."

"After the second drink, Gabelli suffers a massive heart attack and dies."

"Wouldn't he be panicking beforehand as his heart started to race?"

"Sure. Stewart probably talked him down, maybe pretends to call an ambulance."

I said, "Okay, now the body is on the couch or the floor. What does Stewart do next?"

"We know where Gabelli was found. Why don't we work it backward?"

"Good idea, but before we move on, are we even sure he got the heart attack at Stewart's?"

Vargas said, "Stewart needed a place where they could have a couple of drinks. That could be anywhere, but more than that, he needed a private place where he could either dump the meds in his drink, at least one time, or plunge a needle into Gabelli. Plus, he wouldn't know what the reaction would be. He couldn't count on being able to get Gabelli out of there."

"You're right, most likely this happened in Stewart's place."

"So how does he get the body to Clam Pass?"

"Any thought to whether he sat on the body before dumping him?"

"I doubt it. Unless it didn't happen at his house. Very few people have the stones to sleep in the same house with a person they killed."

"Stones? More like you gotta be out of your mind."

"Assuming he wanted to get rid of the body as fast as possible, he had to use his car to at least get him close to the water. He may have used a boat afterward, though we have no evidence of that."

"Stewart would've had to move Gabelli down the stairs and into his car."

"He probably wrapped the body in his garage."

Vargas nodded. "Then he waited until sometime in the middle of the night to drive it to Clam Pass."

"I want to take another run at the neighbor who said he borrowed Stewart's car."

"Sure. You know, Stewart could have went in another way. We've got miles and miles of waterways. He could've put him on a boat somewhere, even on one of those streets in Seagate. They all have water access."

"I'm hoping we don't have to prove that part. Stewart had an affair with the deceased's wife. She says he wanted it to continue. We know he threatened other guys who were with Robin. If we can tie him to the drug that killed a healthy Gabelli, we've got a lot to work with. And that's before a search. Who knows what else we'll get?"

52

LUCA

Vargas, four uniforms, and I slithered into Calusa Bay and parked our cars in front of Stewart's home. The street was wet from a rain shower, and steam was rising from the asphalt. Before we were halfway up the stairs, two sets of neighbors opened their doors to see what was going on. On the verge of telling them to get a life, I pushed the bell instead.

Stewart opened the door, and I thrust the warrant at him.

"Mr. Stewart, this is a search warrant authorized by Judge Randolph. It allows us to search your property and seize anything we believe is related to our case."

"What case?"

"The murder of Philip Gabelli."

Stewart started to breathe rapidly. "What do I have to do with that?"

"Step aside, Mr. Stewart, we are going to conduct our search."

Stewart thrust his hand into his pocket and I drew my weapon. Vargas grabbed his arm and said, "Take your hand out slowly."

Stewart followed her instructions while gasping for breath. "It's only my inhaler. I need my inhaler."

Vargas dug into his pocket and came out with a blue inhaler. She read the label, shook her head, and gave it to Stewart.

I said, "Mr. Stewart, you stay in the foyer with Officer Putnak."

Stewart wheezed. "You're detaining me?"

"During the course of executing a search warrant the court allows us to control the inhabitants of the property in question."

He pulled his inhaler out of his mouth. "Control?"

Even though he was sucking away on his inhaler, he was fighting back.

Vargas said, "Mr. Stewart, the law is clear. If you resist we will have to put you under arrest. Is that clear?"

Stewart stepped aside and we spilled into his house. Pulling on gloves, I told an officer to make sure Stewart stayed out of the way and in the foyer.

Vargas whispered, "The inhaler's a natural product called Dr. Kings. It's over the counter."

"Okay, I'll take the master. You check the kitchen and living room and have the officers search the garage."

Stewart's bedroom was colorless. It wasn't one of those modern white themes; it was a dull, old-looking white. The place was crying for color. I drew the silhouette shades and went straight to the nightstand. My methodology was to open the bottom drawer first and work my way up, leaving each drawer open so I'd know it'd been searched.

The bottom drawer had a dusty pair of binoculars and two old flip phones with dead batteries that I decided to leave there. Inside the second drawer was a thick photo album and about fifteen pairs of neatly folded socks. I pulled the album out and leafed through images of Stewart as a child, teenager, and adult. No one else appeared in the eighty or so photos except you-know-who. I pulled out the picture of Robin and turned it over, but there were no notations.

Staring at the photo, I understood Stewart's fascination. Wearing a red midriff blouse and the tiniest of shorts, Robin was reclined poolside at the Gabelli house. No doubt, she had the goods. After capturing a cell phone image of the photo, I moved to the top drawer.

Sliding it open, a surge of adrenaline coursed through my body. I walked over to the doorway and stuck my head in.

"Hey, Vargas. You got a second?"

I was snapping pictures of the open drawer when my partner came in.

"What's up?"

I put a finger to my lips and pointed to three bottles of terbutaline and a box of hypodermics needles sitting to the right of a watch and coin dish.

Vargas whispered, "We got him, Frank, we got him."

"I think so. But no champagne yet. Continue looking, we may get lucky."

After noting the pharmacy name and the prescribing doctor, I closed the drawer, then continued searching the master suite. There was nothing else that seemed to matter.

Entering the living room, I said, "Bag all the seat cushions."

Stewart said, "You can't take all of them. Where am I gonna sit?"

Vargas pulled me aside and whispered, "We're not supposed to take anything like that. The warrant's scope does not provide for that. What are you looking for?"

"Bodily fluids. If he killed him here, maybe Gabelli leaked when he passed."

"You know we need cause, Frank."

"Okay, just take the left couch cushion."

"You sure, Frank? We've got nothing to justify it."

I pointed to a photo of Gabelli and Stewart sitting on the couch.

"That's really going out on a limb, Frank."

I smiled. "Maybe, but Gabelli's got a red shirt on, same as the day he went missing. Bag the photo as well and give Stewart a receipt for what we took."

"Uh, Detective Luca?"

"Yes, this is Detective Frank Luca. Who is this?"

"Uh, my name's Lenny, Lenny Nership, you came to see me. I live across from Dom."

I looked at the phone before saying, "Yes. Of course, I remember. You're the neighbor who said you borrowed Mr. Stewart's car."

"I, I don't know how to say this but . . . I hope I don't get in trouble or anything. I didn't mean anything, he said it was . . ."

"Take it easy. No one's going to get in any trouble. Just tell me what's on your mind."

"Well, I never borrowed Dom's car."

"The white Nissan Cube?"

"Yeah. He asked me to say I did, but I didn't."

"I see. Now, what made you lie to the police? And don't worry, it's nothing to worry about."

"Well, you see, he said he was having an affair with the sheriff's wife, and he knew the cops were watching him."

"You never borrowed Mr. Stewart's car last May?"

"No, sir."

"Can I ask what made you call today?"

"Well, I love to watch *CSI*, the Miami one, and I know what it looks like when the police do a search warrant. I saw when you all went to Dom's house. I figured he did something really bad, so I called him to see what was happening. He said it was a misunderstanding, but it didn't make sense. Then I started thinking, and I googled the sheriff to see what his wife looked like, but she was like not so pretty and kinda old, a lot older than Dom. So, I started to think that I had to say something."

"That was very smart of you."

"I, I'm afraid, though, that if he finds out he'll go off on me."

"Rest assured, he'll never find out. You see, we'll tell him we have video of him leaving Calusa Bay that night."

"You sure?"

"Yes. Now we'll need to get a statement from you. Is that okay?"

"Uh, do I have to?"

This was a job for Vargas; she'd disarm him. "Yes, it will be quick. I'm going to send my partner. She's a nice lady. Her name's Mary Ann. Please tell her exactly what you told me."

After hanging up, I fist-pumped. Definitely time to haul Stewart in.

53

LUCA

I DECIDED TO USE THE SMALLEST INTERROGATION ROOM WE had. Stewart had asthma, and the size of the room would make him uncomfortable. He'd hemmed and hawed when we asked him to come in, but the veiled threat that we'd arrest him convinced him to come in voluntarily. That was a good thing, because we only had circumstantial evidence.

Vargas and I had settled on a strategy, now it was time to see where it would bring us. We had Stewart escorted into the room and left him alone for fifteen minutes while we got some coffee.

I peered into the one-way window. Stewart was drumming a thumb on the steel table, appearing defiant. I had raised the thermometer just before he was put in the room. When I adjusted the temperature even higher, Vargas shook her head and left to go to the lady's room.

By the time she got back, Stewart had spread his elbows on the table. It was showtime. I gave a quick knock and we entered.

"Mr. Stewart, thank you for coming in today. You remember my partner, Mary Ann Vargas?"

Stewart shook his head. "It's like an oven in here."

"It does seem a tad warm. Would you like it cooler?"

"Absolutely."

"No problem. Mary Ann will lower the thermostat while I set up the video."

"Video?"

"It's standard practice. It's for your protection."

"Yeah, right, my protection."

"It is, trust me. Think about it, this way the record is straight. There's no my word against yours. We can't make up anything. It's all documented."

Vargas came back in. "I set it at seventy-two. It feels better in here already."

Stewart said, "Thank you."

We settled into plastic chairs opposite Stewart, and Vargas turned on the recording device. After she stated the occupants, time, and date, I began the interview.

"Mr. Stewart, the night Philip Gabelli went missing, your Nissan Cube was observed in Clam Pass Park in the middle of the night. When we questioned you about it, you told us that you had loaned the car to a neighbor."

"That's right."

"And who was that neighbor?"

Stewart pulled out his inhaler. "Lenny Nership."

"That's funny, because he said that you asked him to say he borrowed it that night."

"He's lying. Something's wrong with that guy. I feel bad for him, but he's missing a chromosome or something."

"Why would he lie about something like that?"

Stewart shrugged. "I don't know, but why would I ask him to say that?"

Vargas said, "To keep you away from where the body was found."

"Yeah, right. You think I killed my best buddy?"

"We're just trying to understand what you were doing at Clam Pass that night."

Stewart took a hit on his inhaler. "Maybe I got the nights mixed up. Maybe I was on a date."

"With who?"

"Probably somebody I met at Campiello's."

"You don't remember?"

Stewart smiled. "I don't want to brag, but I do okay with the ladies."

"But not with Robin."

Anger flashed across Stewart's face. "What's that supposed to mean?"

"Nothing. Just saying."

Vargas said, "I see you use an inhaler. You suffer from asthma, right?"

"Yeah, had it since I was a little kid."

"It's tough. When I was a kid, Katie, my best friend, had it and it was tough at times."

"I do fine managing it. It doesn't keep me from doing what I want."

"I guess all the drugs they have these days makes it easier to manage."

I thought I saw Stewart flinch before he said, "Guess so."

I said, "You know your buddy Phil, he died of a heart attack."

"A heart attack?"

"Yup."

Stewart started breathing through his mouth. "That's crazy. He was in great shape. I guess you never know what's going on inside your body. It's scary."

Vargas said, "Certainly is."

"That's why I always say you gotta live your life to the

fullest. Better to be king of the hill while you can, because you never know when it's your time to go."

I found myself nodding. What Stewart said rang true to me and I drifted off. Vargas kneed me under the table as she said, "Something's bothering me. Phil Gabelli suffered a massive heart attack that caused his death. So why and how did he end up in Clam Pass?"

I said, "Yeah, why would someone make it look like a murder?"

Stewart said, "There's a lot of twisted people out there."

Vargas said, "But that's what his was."

I said, "What do you think, Dom?"

"He could've been doing a lot of coke and his heart gave out. The guys or girls he was with panicked and they got rid of his body."

All suspects who turn out to be guilty have a couple of scenarios ready to roll off their tongues. Shows they had things all thought out, or so they thought.

Vargas said, "That's good. What do you think, Frank?"

I pawed my chin. "I like it except for one thing."

Vargas said, "What's that?"

"It wasn't coke that killed Gabelli, but terbutaline."

Stewart said, "Turt, what?"

"Nice try, Dom. But you know exactly what terbutaline is. Right, Mary Ann?"

Vargas said, "We found the drug at your home during our search, and subsequent inquires confirm you have been prescribed it for over ten years."

I said, "Ring a bell now?"

"You mean the little bottles? I only use that in emergencies when my inhaler doesn't work, like during allergy season."

"Or when you want to do away with a buddy."

"That's bullshit!"

Vargas said, "We find it interesting that you asked your doctor for more terbutaline a month before Philip Gabelli was murdered."

"It was allergy season. That's why I asked, if you want to know."

Stewart took a hit on his inhaler as Vargas said, "Mr. Stewart, what we know is, you are in possession of ample amounts of the drug that caused Mr. Gabelli to suffer a massive cardiac arrest. And the interesting angle is, you were sleeping with the victim's wife."

I said, "Not really, she tossed him aside after a quickie. Maybe he's not as good in the sack as he thinks he is."

"Screw you."

I said, "So, tell us, how'd you do it, Dom?"

"I didn't do anything."

I said, "Look, we can dance around as long as you want, but we know you did it, and you're going down for it."

Stewart panted as he stared at his hands.

Vargas said, "If you cooperate we'll put in a good word with the DA for you. You may be able to work out a plea deal without going to court. You save the taxpayers the expense of a trial, and they will cut you some slack on the jail term."

Stewart raised his head. "I'm through talking. I want my attorney."

———————

"I CAN'T BELIEVE they cut Stewart loose."

"Come on, Frank. You knew we didn't have enough to hold him."

"Okay then, you tell me: One, how many people take

terbutaline; two, who knew Gabelli; three, slept with his wife; four, sent us on wild-goose chases?"

"Circumstantial, all of it. Don't forget, he had a valid script for the drug. I hate to admit it, but his attorney was right. It's not a crime to be prescribed a drug that could be used in lethal quantities. And he's never been in trouble before."

"There's a first time for everything, and this is it. We just need a piece of physical evidence and Stewart's done."

"Whatever happened with the cushion from the search?"

I said, "Nothing, no bodily fluids or traces of terbutaline."

"I think it works to our advantage that Stewart thinks he's in the clear."

"I don't like it. You look up the word smug in the dictionary and there's a picture of Stewart."

"Wasn't it you who taught me not to get personal but to work harder?"

I nodded. "You're right. Look, while he's parading around like a free bird, we'll redouble our efforts. Let's start by canvassing Stewart's neighborhood, see if anyone can remember seeing Gabelli there the night Stewart went to Clam Pass. See if anyone remembers Stewart leaving in the middle of the night, somebody out walking their dog or something. Anything we get, even circumstantial, will help dial up the heat on him."

Vargas said, "Sounds like a plan. Still nothing on Stewart's old car?"

"Nah. The dealer kept it on his lot for a couple of months and it didn't move, so they sold it at an auction in Georgia. A wholesaler out of Pennsylvania picked it up and he had it for a month before he sold it to a dealer in Massachusetts. Anyway, they're running it down, though. We should have something soon."

"I'm not hopeful. Stewart seems careful, though he screwed up with the neighbor borrowing the car thing."

"Maybe, but the neighbor had borrowed the Cube a couple of times. He could've gotten the dates mixed up."

"But the line about him having an affair with the sheriff's wife, what's up with that?"

I shook my head. "We need a little break, that's all, and we're way overdue for one."

54

SOMERVILLE POLICE OFFICERS CROWLEY AND SPEAR PULLED up to 81 Gilead Street. They climbed out of their car and peered down the driveway to the home. The officers nodded to each other and climbed the rickety stairs of the early nineteenth-century home. They knocked on the door, and a woman in her late forties, wearing gym clothes and eating a banana, opened the door. The officers introduced themselves and asked, "Ma'am, do you own a white Nissan Cube, year 2010?"

The color drained out of the woman's face. "Yes, it's my son's car. Why?"

Officer Crowley handed a slip of paper to the woman. "We have a seizure warrant. We're here to collect the car."

She leaned against the doorframe, dropping her banana. "What did he do?"

"We don't believe he did anything. The car is wanted in connection with a case involving a previous owner."

"It has nothing to do with us?"

"Don't believe so, ma'am."

"Oh, thank God."

A tow truck rumbled to a stop in front of the house.

"We're going to need to take the car."

"When will we get it back? He needs the car for school. He's in college, you know."

"We'll give you a receipt after we've loaded it on the truck, and there's a contact number on it. You can call that number later today. They'll provide you with all the details."

Neighbors had gathered in the street to witness the loading of the Nissan onto the tow truck. As the truck ambled its way out of view, the mother went around to her neighbors, explaining the unusual circumstances.

55

LUCA

Stewart raised his handcuffed hands. "You going to take these off?"

I originally wanted to cuff his hands behind his back, but Vargas reminded me he needed access to his inhaler. Keeping a prisoner in cuffs was a controversial tactic I'd never used. With Stewart, I was betting it would help break him down. We're in control, not you, Dom.

I said, "New security rules. Can't take 'em off. But what I can do is cuff one arm to the table if you'd like."

"Do it then."

I told Vargas to get things going, and she stated the formalities for the record while I rearranged the shackles.

I sat down next to Vargas. "Mr. Stewart, were you at Clam Pass the night of Philip Gabelli's disappearance?"

"I might have been. It was a long time ago."

"We have video footage of your white Nissan Cube in the parking lot."

"Like I said, it was a long time ago."

"Previously you've stated that because it was the night

Gabelli went missing, you had, how did he say it, Detective Vargas?"

Vargas said, "I believe it was crystal-clear recollection."

I said, "That was it. If you'd like, we can play it back for you."

Stewart said, "Things were stressful. I could've been there that night on a date."

I said, "So, we're back to the date excuse."

"It's not an excuse."

Vargas said, "Did your date meet you there?"

Where was she going? I could tell by Stewart's face he was just as confused as I was.

"What do you mean, meet me there? Is this some kinda police trick?"

Vargas said, "It's not a trick question, Mr. Stewart. It's a simple question. Did your date meet you at Clam Pass Park?"

"No, we left Campiello's, I think it was, and went to the park together."

"That's interesting," Vargas said.

"What's so interesting?"

Vargas said, "The tape we have clearly indicates you were alone in the Nissan Cube when you entered the parking lot."

What? Vargas was bluffing. I loved it, but if Stewart's attorney got wind of it she'd have some explaining to do.

"I don't know what you're trying to prove, Detective. So what if I went by myself?"

I said, "Then what were you doing at Clam Pass at that time of night?"

"Couldn't sleep, went for a walk."

I said, "You should try keeping your story straight. It doesn't look good when you keep changing things."

Vargas said, "I know, a walk helps me to sleep. So, you were at Clam Pass that night going for a walk?"

Stewart nodded and took a deep hit off his inhaler.

Vargas said, "Mr. Stewart, could you please speak your answer."

"I was there, but big deal. You're gonna need more than that to pin Phil's murder on me."

"Funny you should say that, isn't it, Mary Ann?"

Vargas said, "I don't know how funny Mr. Stewart will find it, but you want to tell him, or shall I?"

I hated to give up a kill shot, but she'd done a masterful job setting him up. I said, "Be my guest."

Vargas steepled her hands and drummed them for a full twenty seconds. Stewart's shoulders sunk with each repetition. I had to clear my throat to get her moving.

Vargas said, "What we *do* have, Mr. Stewart, is solid forensic evidence that Philip Gabelli was in your Nissan Cube."

Stewart bolted upright. "You guys are geniuses, you know that?" He smiled. "Of course, there's some of Phil's DNA, or whatever, in my car. You forget, we were best friends. He's been in my car dozens of times, and hey, for the record, I've been in his car a lot too."

I said, "Detective Vargas is smarter than me, but it doesn't take a genius to catch a killer. Just old-fashioned police work and a dash of the sciences."

Stewart's eyes blinked rapidly as he wet his lips.

Vargas said, "Can you explain how Philip Gabelli's urine and blood were found in your car?"

"The guy pissed in my car?"

I said, "Upon his death, Mr. Gabelli released a small amount of urine that was found on your passenger seat."

"That's crazy. Phil could've leaked some anytime, like when we stopped on the way to the casino."

"And the blood found in the passenger foot well?"

"I don't know, a bloody nose?"

"Very good. Terbutaline dramatically raises the blood pressure, resulting in nosebleeds. The capillary hemorrhages found in Mr. Gabelli's nasal cavity are consistent with a nosebleed."

"You're grasping at straws."

Vargas said, "I afraid you're wrong, Mr. Stewart. Did you know that the discharge of fluids from a dead person is chemically different from that of a living person?"

Stewart stiffened.

What did she just say? I had to replay it. I was impressed by the crafty way Vargas put it. I said, "You're done, Stewart." I turned to my partner. "You know what, Vargas? I still can't figure out why Robin would even take one roll in the sack with this guy. What do you think?"

Stewart shook his head. "You don't know her like I do. You don't know nothing about her, or me."

I said, "I know Robin's a pretty highbrow girl. An uptowner, we used to call them, up in Jersey. You two have nothing in common."

"We're more alike than you think. She deserved more than Phil gave her. Man, he treated her like dirt. How could he do that to her? She has it all."

I said, "Robin's a smart, accomplished woman. A professional, earning the big wood. If you two even had something at one time, and I doubt it, it would never have lasted. You're Single-A, Stewart, Double-A at best. She's in the majors."

Stewart smiled. "You're clueless. Robin told me we were soul mates, that nobody understood her like I did. We had a special connection."

I said, "Only when she needed you. Don't you get it? Robin used you. She was feeling lonely. You were her teddy bear for one night. That was the extent of it."

Stewart sucked greedily on his inhaler and I continued.

"You know what she told us, Dom? Robin said she immediately regretted having a one-time thing with you."

"No way she said that."

Vargas said, "It's true. I was there when she said it."

"That's not what she told me after we were together. She said it was special."

"She was lying to you, Dom. She despised you, hated the way you shadowed her every move. Right, Mary Ann?"

Vargas said, "The way Robin put it was that you were suffocating her."

"Suffocating her? That's bullshit. I don't know why she turned on me. Robin and me were perfect together. Phil was nothing but a drain on her. He sucked the life out of her and pissed away her money to boot. I'd never do that to her. I'd take care of her, protect her. We wouldn't need anything from anybody. We'd have it all. Look at her house, man, what a place to live, and you know what? I almost made it. My plan was good."

I said, "Tell us about the plan, Dom."

Vargas said, "You know, we did a lot of investigating, and there's no doubt Phil Gabelli was a terrible husband."

Stewart said, "Tell me about it. First, I tried to get Phil to leave. I tried reasoning with him, but he was stubborn. And Robin, I don't know why the hell she didn't walk away. She was being made a fool of. Over and over again."

I said, "Even the people she worked with knew he was running after every skirt. It was embarrassing for her."

Stewart said, "It was sickening. She should have begged me to get him out of the way."

Vargas said, "Maybe if she knew it was you who got her cheating husband out of the way, she would've seen things differently."

"You think so?"

Vargas said, "Absolutely. I'm a woman, and I know how Robin thinks."

Stewart shoulders slumped. "I never thought about telling her, but it was still a good plan."

I said, "It was a brilliant plan. We just about gave up on catching you."

Vargas said, "Why don't you tell us about it?"

Stewart revealed that he began crafting his plan after Phil embarrassed him in front of a woman he was making headway with. Plan finalized, Stewart decided to implement it after a night in a pool hall when Phil disappeared with a floozy into a bathroom. After the sexual encounter, Phil further infuriated Stewart by bad-mouthing Robin to a bunch of guys in a billiards tournament. The combo compelled Stewart to hatch the plan.

The deadly plot wasn't exactly like we thought, but we were close. Stewart invited Gabelli over to watch a hockey playoff game, and in preparation had crushed a handful of pills that morning. He then dissolved some of the powder into each of the two vodka and cranberry drinks Gabelli had. His heart racing, Gabelli panicked, and Stewart said he'd take him to the hospital.

They got in Stewart's Cube, which was in the garage. Stewart had two hypodermic needles loaded with terbutaline in the car and sank both of them into Gabelli's thigh at the same time. Gabelli never knew what hit him and quickly succumbed to cardiac arrest.

Gabelli dead, Stewart reclined the seat and slipped plastic around the body. Then he dumped Gabelli's car in Lehigh Acres and waited a couple of hours before dumping the body into Outer Clam Bay.

We clarified a couple of points to be sure we had him cold before wrapping things up.

AFTER STEWART WAS SHOWN to his cell, Vargas and I met with the district attorney, handing over the confession and evidence we'd collected. It was supposed to feel good getting a psycho like Stewart off the street, but it left me unsettled. If you weren't safe with a lifelong friend, where could you be safe?

There's a Gulf of Mexico difference between remorse and regret. Stewart showed zero signs of remorse, just regret that his scheme was rejected by Robin. I knew this nut would shift into a bargaining position to plea his way to a shorter sentence, but he'd get no help from this detective.

I looked forward to a walk on the beach. It always helped to process things after a case like this but before hitting the sand, there were two things I had to do. One, I looked forward to, the other had me rattled. Kayla had said she was free next weekend, which was perfect, as it was Vargas's turn to be on call. I'd love to take a day off and make it a Thursday to Sunday trip but would that be pushing things too fast? We hadn't seen each other since the night at Baleen's when I passed out. And that was our first date.

Realizing my mind had moved things further than they really were, I limited the search for flights and a hotel to the weekend. After checking, it took me longer than expected to compose a text to Kayla before booking anything.

Nervous she'd disappoint me, I headed up the stairs to see Sheriff Liberi, who'd been diagnosed with lymphoma. Liberi and I respected each other and had developed a good relationship. He handled the responsibilities of the office flawlessly and had gone out of his way to help me adjust when I joined the department. It was disappointing to learn he was thinking of retiring to confront his illness.

The Sheriff was shaken by the diagnosis and who could blame him? If anyone could emphasize, it was me. I felt a duty to try and settle him down but the idea of talking about things I hadn't yet put to bed, made me skittish. As I exited the stairwell, the fear I wouldn't be up to the task began to creep into my head.

Ducking into the men's room, I began rehearsing a couple of lines I'd tell Liberi when my phone chimed. It was a text from Kayla. I opened the text and exhaled, the weekend was on. The news heartened me, providing the courage to comfort and support a friend. I sent a smiley to Kayla and went to see the Sheriff.

THE NEXT BOOK in this series is, The Serenity Murder. Find it in eBook, Paperback, and Audio.

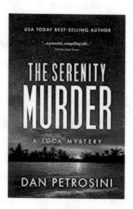

I sincerely hope you enjoyed reading this book as much

as I enjoyed writing it. If you did, I would greatly appreciate a short review on Amazon or your favorite book website. Reviews are crucial for any author, and even just a line or two can make a huge difference. Thank you, Dan.

Visit Dan's Website: http://danpetrosini.com/

OTHER BOOKS BY DAN

THE LUCA MYSTERY SERIES

Am I the Killer

Vanished

The Serenity Murder

Third Chances

A Cold, Hard Case

Cop or Killer?

Silencing Salter

A Killer Missteps

Uncertain Stakes

The Grandpa Killer

Dangerous Revenge

Where Are They

Buried at the Lake

The Preserve Killer

No One is Safe

SUSPENSEFUL SECRETS

Cory's Dilemma

Cory's Flight

Cory's Shift

OTHER WORKS BY DAN PETROSINI

The Final Enemy

Complicit Witness

Push Back

Ambition Cliff

ABOUT THE AUTHOR

Dan is a USA Today and Amazon best-selling author who wrote his first story at the age of ten and enjoys telling a story or joke.

Dan gets his story ideas by exploring the question; What if?

In almost every situation he finds himself in, Dan explores what if this or that happened? What if this person died or did something unusual or illegal?

Dan's non-stop mind spin provides him with plenty of material to weave into interesting stories.

A fan of books and films that have twists and are difficult to predict, Dan crafts his stories to prevent readers from guessing correctly. He writes every day, forcing the words out when necessary and has written over twenty-five novels to date.

It's not a matter of wanting to write, Dan simply has to.

Dan passionately believes people can realize their dreams if they focus and act, and he encourages just that.

His favorite saying is – "The price of discipline is always less than the cost of regret"

Dan reminds people to get the negativity out of their lives. He believes it is contagious and advises people to steer clear of negative people. He knows having a true, positive mind set makes it feel like life is rigged in your favor. When he gets off base, he tells himself, 'You can't have a good day with a bad attitude.'

Married with two daughters and a needy Maltese, Dan lives in Southwest Florida. A New York native, Dan has taught at local colleges, writes novels, and plays tenor saxophone in several jazz bands. He also drinks way too much wine and never, ever takes himself too seriously.

He puts out a twice-a-month newsletter featuring articles, his writing and special deals and steals.

Sign up at www.danpetrosini.com

CPSIA information can be obtained
at www.ICGtesting.com
Printed in the USA
LVHW050153120723
752249LV00011B/499

9 781960 286048